PENGUIN BOOKS

ASTRID & VERONIKA

LINDA OLSSON was born in Stockholm, Sweden. She graduated from the University of Stockholm with a Bachelor of Law, then pursued a career in banking and finance until she left Sweden in 1986. She has lived in Kenya, Singapore, Britain and Japan and has been a permanent resident in New Zealand since 1990. In 1993 she completed a Bachelor of Arts in English and German literature at Victoria University of Wellington. In 2003 she won the *Sunday Star-Times* Short Story Competition. She lives in Auckland and this is her first novel.

ASTRID

&

VERONIKA

Linda Olsson

PENGUIN BOOKS

PENGUIN BOOKS

Published by the Penguin Group

Penguin Group (USA) Inc., 375 Hudson Street, New York, New York 10014, U.S.A.
Penguin Group (Canada), 90 Eglinton Avenue East, Suite 700, Toronto,
Ontario, Canada M4P 2Y3 (a division of Pearson Penguin Canada Inc.)
Penguin Books Ltd, 80 Strand, London WC2R 0RL, England
Penguin Ireland, 25 St Stephen's Green, Dublin 2, Ireland
(a division of Penguin Books Ltd)
Penguin Group (Australia), 250 Camberwell Road, Camberwell,
Victoria 3124, Australia (a division of Pearson Australia Group Pty Ltd)
Penguin Books India Pvt Ltd, 11 Community Centre,
Panchsheel Park, New Delhi – 110 017, India
Penguin Group (NZ), cnr Airborne and Rosedale Roads, Albany,
Auckland 1310, New Zealand (a division of Pearson New Zealand Ltd)
Penguin Books (South Africa) (Pty) Ltd, 24 Sturdee Avenue,
Rosebank, Johannesburg 2196, South Africa

Penguin Books Ltd, Registered Offices:
80 Strand, London WC2R 0RL, England

First published in New Zealand under the title
Let Me Sing You Gentle Songs by Penguin Books (NZ) 2005
Published in Penguin Books (USA) 2007

1   3   5   7   9   10   8   6   4   2

Pages 259–267 constitute an extension of this copyright page.

PUBLISHER'S NOTE
This is a work of fiction. Names, characters, places, and incidents are either the product
of the author's imagination or are used fictitiously, and any resemblance to actual persons,
living or dead, business establishments, events, or locales is entirely coincidental.

LIBRARY OF CONGRESS CATALOGING-IN-PUBLICATION DATA
Olsson, Linda.
[Let me sing you gentle songs]
Astrid & Veronika / Linda Olsson
p.   cm.
Originally published under title: Let me sing you gentle songs
ISBN 978-0-14-303807-8
1. Female friendship—Fiction.   2. Sweden—Fiction.
I. Title.   II. Title: Astrid and Veronika.
PR9639.4.O47   2007
823'.912—dc22   2006050660

Printed in the United States of America
Set in Whitman

For Anna-Lisa, my grandmother, my friend

I drift around my rooms and write
to shadows, thinking as I always did,
that writing only can make peace, can right
and heal that which a life made sordid.

BO BERGMAN, 'Sömnlös' (Sleepless) in
Äventyret (*The adventure*), 1969

ASTRID

&

VERONIKA

PROLOGUE

Astrid

July 1942, Västra Sångeby, Dalarna, Sweden

When the sun dipped behind the wall of trees, we lay down
and the white night swallowed us. It has been night ever
since.

Veronika

November 2002, Karekare, New Zealand

Above us the pitiless sun, while the world swirled
incomprehensible around the stillness that was the two of us.
Then the violent crashing of the victorious sea.

1

. . . as the day breaks.

There had been wind and drifting snow during her journey, but as darkness fell, the wind died and the snow settled.

It was the first day of March. She had driven from Stockholm in the gradually deepening dusk that seamlessly became night. It had been a slow journey, but it had given her time to think. Or erase thoughts.

She turned off the main road by the church, then on to the narrow steep road up the hill, and took the last turn on to the unsealed road. No cars had passed here since the new snow had fallen and the road had a pristine soft whiteness between the rounded banks of packed snow. She drove slowly, her eyes adjusting to the darkness. She had been told there were only two houses up here, and she saw them outlined against the sky. Both lay dark; there were no lights anywhere.

She passed the larger house and, further along, left the road altogether, driving through the snow into the front yard of the second house. She parked near the steps leading up to the porch. A path had been cleared in preparation for her arrival, but new snow had fallen since and it was now just a soft indent in the white blanket. When she stepped out of the car, she saw stalks of dead grass sticking through the snow, and there were icy patches just underneath. Being careful not to slip, she trod cautiously as she moved back and forth between car and house, emptying the boot and back seat. The only sound as she carried bags and boxes into the house was the brittle crunching of snow under her feet. She kept the headlights on and the light slanted across her footprints in the snow.

The neighbouring house was a silent shadow, looming in the darkness beyond the tunnel of light where she walked. The air was dry and cold and her breath left her lips in whiffs of white vapour dissolving in the night. The sky was a black infinity without stars or moon. She felt as if she had dropped through a tunnel into a world of absolute silence.

That night, she lay in a bed where her body was an unfamiliar shape, in this house that didn't know her yet. In the silent darkness, it was as if she were nowhere. She felt light as air.

Next morning the sun was barely able to penetrate a white sky. She opened the window to a light wind and the possibility of more snow in the air. She stood looking out, pulling her red bathrobe tight over her chest. She thought about her journey, but refused to let her mind follow the road back to the starting point. Instead, she thought about the many journeys before. Unpacking in unfamiliar places, making a home wherever a certain journey ended, with her father the only constant. She knew that this journey was different. All her life she had travelled in his company, her hand in her father's, on their way towards a new overseas posting. Since her mother left it had always been the two of them. And somehow, even the most exotic place had become just another stop on their journey together. But the father she had visited in Tokyo in December now had his own life, separate from hers. They were no longer fellow travellers. This journey was a solitary one. A flight, an escape. A journey without a goal. Her life felt as uncertain as the light. Poised in a white nothingness.

She closed the window but remained standing, looking out. She could see beyond the river and the village, into the blue distance of forests and mountains. The landscape before her seemed ancient, rounded mountains polished by ice and wind, slow-moving rivers and still lakes. It was land that provided sparingly, and only after hard toil.

She turned and looked across the field. What had been in shadow the evening before was now starkly exposed in the bleak morning light. The other house was larger than it had seemed: a generous two-storey wooden building that might once have been painted yellow but was now fading into indistinct pale grey, blending in with the colours of the sky and the snow. The windows were empty black squares. Still no signs of life.

There was firewood in a basket by the stove, thoughtfully prepared with fine dry sticks on top and larger pieces underneath. She decided to make a fire, and she also turned on the electric cooker to heat water for a coffee. She sat at the table with the mug between her hands while the fire slowly began to crackle.

She had arrived without a timeframe and had brought only a few bags with her personal belongings, books and CDs. The decision had been sudden, leaving little time for preparations. In fact it hadn't been so much a decision as a series of almost unconscious swift actions. She felt she had no plans, no thoughts; yet at some level, her mind and her body had taken action and catapulted her into this pool of stillness.

By the second day the house still kept its distance. There were signs of recent renovation — new wallpaper, new bathroom fittings and tiles. New cupboards in the kitchen, smart and practical but a little out of place. It was a modest, unassuming house with an abandoned quality about it. Minimally furnished, with a table and six chairs in the kitchen, two small sofas and a coffee table in the sitting room, and two beds in the upstairs bedroom. The wooden floors were crisscrossed by strips of hand-loomed rag rugs and the windows had no curtains, just plain white blinds. She hadn't bothered to have the telephone connected, but she had brought her mobile. She kept it turned off, in the drawer of the bedside table.

She was an orphan tenant in an orphan house.

Her life slowly found its own organic rhythm. After a week she had established her morning routine. She got up early, had coffee at the kitchen table and watched the room absorb the growing daylight. It felt as if the house had accepted her, as if they had begun their life together. The soles of her feet had become familiar with the wooden steps of the staircase, her nose accustomed to the smells of the walls, and she was gradually adding her own imprint, leaving minute traces. She shifted the sofas around in the sitting room so she could sit and look out the window, and she bought a potted geranium for the kitchen windowsill. She had created a workplace of sorts on one end of the kitchen table: the laptop stood open, ready to register words; her notebook, dictionaries and pens were neatly stacked on one side. Fingers poised on the keys, she spent time staring into the screen, but what little writing she did, she erased again.

Each day began with a walk, regardless of the weather. Unless she walked all the way down to the village, she rarely saw another person. One morning, a deer stood watching as she walked across the front yard. It remained there, still, its eyes locking with hers, before soundlessly turning and disappearing behind the barn in one swift movement. She saw the tracks of moose and foxes in the snow. The nights were still cold, and in the darkness winter reclaimed what had been conceded during the days. Each morning began grey and icy.

The house across the field remained dark and silent. For the first few days she wasn't sure whether it was inhabited. Then one day she exchanged a few words with the woman at the checkout in the village shop and introduced herself.

'I am Veronika Bergman. I'm renting the Malms' house up on the hill.'

'Ah, so you are Astrid's new neighbour,' the woman replied. She smiled and rolled her eyes. 'Astrid Mattson, the village witch. Doesn't like people. Keeps to herself. Not much of a neighbour, I'm afraid.' She handed Veronika her change, then added, 'As you will discover, no doubt.'

It was two weeks before she saw her neighbour for the first time. The old woman looked almost obscenely exposed, a hunched solitary figure in a dark heavy coat and rubber boots, uncertainly navigating the icy road on her way to the village. Her house had been her protector until then, the dark windows loyal keepers of the secrets of the life inside.

After her daily walk, Veronika sat down in front of the laptop, but her eyes drifted from the screen to the window

5

and the landscape beyond. There had been a time when she had felt that the book was absolutely clear, perfectly shaped in her mind, and that the process of typing the words would be a mere technical exercise, swift and easy. That all that was required was her withdrawal from the world, and she would see. Stillness. Peace.

But the screen remained blank.

The grey weather prevailed. It was as if time stood still. It didn't snow, but nor was there any sun. Invisible crows cawed in an otherwise silent world.

One morning, as she passed by her neighbour's house on her daily walk, she noticed that the kitchen window was open. It was just a chink, wide enough for someone to look out, but offering no view of the interior. Veronika waved as she walked past. She imagined the old woman there, in the darkness behind the glass, but she couldn't be sure.

She was thinking about the book, about the continuous process of reshaping and reassembling all her ideas and plans. It was as if the book she had begun in another world, in another life, had been written by someone else. The words no longer had a connection with the person she had become. Here, there were no distractions other than those she carried within, and everything lay exposed. It was time to find new words.

Then, finally, the promise of spring. Veronica stood on the porch and looked up into a sky that was an endless blue canvas, with a flight of migrating birds like delicate drifting black calligraphy. The morning had dawned with no hint of a change and she had cut short her morning walk. Now, with the sun on her face, she decided to walk down to the river.

She strolled down the hill, crossed the road and carried on through the stretch of forest. Grainy snow still piled in the shade at the foot of the firs, but down at the river the ice was breaking, sending large chunks bobbing on the dark surface. The spring flood was yet to arrive: the snow in the mountains hadn't begun to melt. She kept her face upturned towards the sun, and when she got back home she sat down on the front steps for a while. The stones were warm under her buttocks. She pulled out her notebook from the small backpack by her side and started to write. When she put down her pen, she was surprised to see that the day was gently folding, the slanting rays of sun filtering through the treetops across the road. She closed the book, lifted her face to the last light and slowly drew a breath.

And realised how long it had been since she had properly filled her lungs.

2

The smallest whirl, a ripple . . .

Astrid stood naked looking out the window. It was late and very dark. If not for the white snow, she wouldn't have been able to see much. Just the yellow eyes of the windows across the field, startled awake after such a long sleep.

Her own house was in darkness, as always. Dark and warm. She kept it well heated. It was an organic part of her and its shapes were ingrained in her body: she navigated the space effortlessly without lights. Also, the darkness sometimes brought the animals close: the moose, the owls, even the lynx. Self-contained observers like her, with their own space, only briefly visiting hers.

She rarely looked out the windows: the view had lost all meaning.

Yet there she was, by the window, enveloped in the warm

darkness of her house, intently following the movements across the white field. She crossed her arms over her chest, cupped her breasts with her hands. They were warm to the touch, heavy. She bent forward, her forehead almost touching the glass. In the stillness of the night all she could see was the dark outline of a woman moving in the bright tunnel of light from the headlights of a car. The front door was wide open, a gaping yellow square in the night. She ran her tongue over her teeth, let it glide over sharp edges and over stretches of soft gum, sucking away the saliva. All the while, she kept her eyes on the other house.

Long after the headlights had been turned off and the front door closed, she remained by the window, embracing herself, letting her hands run over the papery skin of her arms. Staring into the space that separated the houses.

She had expected the arrival, but she was taken by surprise at her own reaction. The fact that she was here, by the window, watching.

The following morning she woke early, as always, in the room behind the kitchen that was her bedroom. She had moved downstairs a long time ago, made her bedroom where once there had been a small dining room. She hadn't made any major changes, just pushed the table up against the window, so that the four chairs on the far side were hard against the wall in order to make room for a narrow bed. She kept her clothes in the hallway outside the kitchen.

There was no blind, only strips of faded chintz pulled back on either side of the window. She liked to wake up in darkness. She dreaded the return of spring and the relentless white nights of summer.

She lay still, watching the shade of the ceiling change, her ears alert. The sounds of darkness were faint but familiar. She could hear the snow adjusting to the slowly rising temperature, the wind preparing to pick up, the rustling of small bodies scuttling across the hard crust of snow that had thawed and frozen over again. The night had folded; the day had arrived. She heard the first sound of morning: the cawing of a crow. As if carried on the light, the sound invaded her room. She didn't move but her eyes were open, her ears sharp. The sound and the light stretched their tentacles around the room, fingered the walls, the ceiling, the floor. Glided over her blanket and paused. She watched the light on the ceiling as the first bleak rays of sun crossed the grey expanse. There was no escape; eventually she must surrender. It was there. She had to concede and begin another day.

Then, just as she put her feet on the floorboards, there was a new sound. She heard a window open, then a door. The sound of steps on icy snow, a car door open, then close again. Sounds of life.

Her morning routine was set and she did not welcome disruptions. The daily regime was not directed by discipline, but for convenience. It allowed her a sense of safety. The days had a pattern, unaffected by the changing seasons. Her life was a matter of sustenance, survival, and her needs were minimal. She made no plans for the future. The garden had gone to seed, the house was crumbling. She knew that the paint was peeling, the chimney cracked. A dying building, housing a dying body.

She walked to the village only when necessary. Especially now in the winter. The roads were rarely cleared up here, where cars had no business, and the melting snow became treacherous ice. She had no fear of death, but wished for it to be on her terms. A broken hip would land her in the hands of those she feared the most. Those who had been waiting for her to need them.

The past was kept at bay. There was no future, and the present was a still void where she existed physically, but with no emotional presence. She waited, her memories kept submerged. The effort was a constant, draining task, absorbing all her energy. And there were moments when it failed. When she was overcome by feelings as intense as when they were new. The triggers were unpredictable and she trod cautiously. For a long time she had drifted in still backwaters, patiently awaiting the final undertow. And now this, a slight rippling of the surface.

She got up and began her day. Washed herself, made coffee. Her kitchen was the same as always, with the old wood stove the centrepiece and an electric cooker on the side. The embers were still alive, needing only a soft breath of air and new wood to rekindle.

She cradled the coffee mug in her hands, sucking on a lump of sugar. When she put the mug down on the kitchen table, her hands absentmindedly stroke the brittle oilcloth, as familiar as her own skin, and brushed off non-existent crumbs. She sat sipping the cooling coffee while a pale sun rose. Her eyes wandered to the window.

Life intruded. Incrementally, it made its way back into her house. Sounds. Windows opening and closing. Faint music through an open window. A car driving off. And she found herself adding them to her daily pattern. As the days went by, observing the house across the field became a central part of her early mornings. She found herself at the table well before the other house stirred, waiting while the shadows of the night withdrew. Her eyes would settle on the upstairs window, where the first signs of life would appear.

She stood by the kitchen window, waiting, until the slight figure emerged from the other house and walked past. She made sure she kept still, well inside the window. Her arms crossed over her chest, embracing herself, she watched the young woman pass by, waving. Then, one morning, she found herself lifting her hand in response. It was a hesitant, slow movement, and as her hand sank she stared at it, as if surprised by its action. She sat down at the table and put both hands in front of her. She opened and closed them several times, then laid them flat, palms down. An old woman's hands, she thought. Translucent, papery skin stretching over raised veins. Liver spots. Yet that split nail on the right little finger, where the soft tip of a five-year-old finger had been caught in the barn door, was intact on the old woman's hand. And the indent at the base of the left ring finger. All those years and it was still there: a permanent, visible scar. A reminder. The mark of her wedding ring.

Her peace had been disturbed. She found herself wandering through the rooms of the house, hands on her lower back. The days were grey, the nights cold. The evenings grew longer and, as she lay awake, hands clasped on her chest, her eyes searching the ceiling over her bed, she listened intently for the new sounds. Muted music escaping through a closed blind. Bed linen shaken out through the upstairs window. The front door opening or closing. Quick steps over the front yard.

She listened and she felt the world invade. Life. And she turned her face to the wall and cried.

Then, on the morning of the first of May, she lay in bed, waiting. The birdsong, the wind were picking up. But no sound from the other house. The room grew lighter; she was ready to rise. But she was still waiting, her ears alert. Later, she sat at the table, her eyes focused on the house across the field. The windows were closed; there was no smoke from the chimney. The car stood silent. She waited.

She opened the window and stood watching. She placed her hands on the kitchen bench and leaned forward, looking out. Only when the cold air filled the kitchen did she close the window.

Two days went by. On the second night she woke and went and stood by the window. The other house lay deathly still. She sat down at the table, looking out. Just as the black night had reached its peak, the dark shapes of two moose gracefully emerged from the solid wall of black trees beyond the open fields. The two animals moved soundlessly over last year's dry grass, the only signs of life in a still world.

Astrid could no longer sleep. She wandered between her room and the kitchen, coffee mug in hand. The car was still in the same place. She couldn't have left. Yet there was no sign of life. She means nothing to me, she told herself. I know nothing about her. I have no business intruding.

She knew nothing more about her neighbour than what she had been able to observe. A young woman. She was no longer sure how to tell age. Twenty-five? Thirty? Slim, with curly dark hair. Short. Not tall, anyway. She had overheard someone talking about her in the shop one day, but as was her habit, she had walked away. Veronika. She had heard the name.

She found herself registering time again. The time of day, the day of the week. Time passed increasingly slowly, and with each passing minute she found it more difficult to tear her eyes away from the other house. It grew to occupy all space, all her thoughts. Eventually, she went and got her jacket.

As she stepped out onto the porch and hesitantly wandered down the gravel path, she was still not fully aware of where her feet were leading her. As when her hand returned the wave, her legs were now acting independently of her conscious mind. She walked down the road and across the front yard of the other house. There were no signs of life. She knocked on the door and stepped back, as if preparing to flee. But when there was no response, she stepped forward and knocked again, harder. She thought she could hear soft sounds, as of bare feet on wooden steps.

When the door opened and she stood face to face with the young woman, she realised that life had irrevocably returned. She cared.

3

. . . tell me, who will save you then?

The day before had been so full of promise, with bright sunshine on the snow. Then, dull and cold again. Veronika sat at the kitchen table sipping tea, watching the wind picking up. There were no colours, just shades of grey and white. The bare trees moved restlessly and snow lifted and swirled in irregular bursts. Time seemed to stand still, poised in a no man's land that was neither winter nor summer.

She had been in the village two months. Finally, she had started to write. It was hard labour, not the rapid process she had anticipated. It was as if the story were a fragile cobweb, and she had to take the utmost care not to rip the thread. The contract and the discussions around the book belonged to another time, as distant as a prehistoric era, and she was struggling to recall her enthusiasm and joy for the project.

Yet words emerged. Painfully, slowly. Unexpected words.

It was the last day of April, Valborgsmäss Eve. The celebration of the end of winter and the beginning of spring. Yet, as always, a bitterly cold day with an icy wind. She had been thinking of making her daily walk a late one so she could go down to the village to watch the bonfire. But she was tired, spring tired. She sat at the kitchen table in front of the laptop. The room was warm — she had lit a fire in the stove — but she still felt cold. The words on the screen in front of her seemed to paint an almost forgotten landscape. It was as if she were slowly unpacking, pulling out one scene after another and exposing them to this bleak light. The effort was enormous. Here, now, each passage seemed out of place, like clothes bought on holiday. Distant and without any connection to her, to this place. She lifted her eyes and looked out the window, but the still landscape seemed withdrawn. She felt as if she were suspended between two worlds, belonging to neither.

The neighbour's house was closed and silent. But the day before, as she had walked past waving, she had noticed that the kitchen window was again ajar, despite the weather. She could have been mistaken, but she thought she saw a movement in the darkness behind the glass. She thought she saw the old woman return her greeting. Today, there was no sign of life.

She shivered and went upstairs to get her fleece jacket. The red one. James's. She pulled it on and sat down again at the table. Unconsciously, her hand stroked the soft material of the sleeve. She lifted her hands to her mouth and blew into them to warm her stiff fingers.

The day drifted into afternoon and she remained in front of the screen, reading more than writing. But as the hours passed the words seemed to withdraw, to blur and rearrange themselves into sequences that became increasingly difficult to decipher. Eventually, she turned off the laptop and closed the lid. The kitchen lay dark; the grey day had deepened into early evening. As she stood she had to support herself with a hand on the table for a moment before crossing the floor. Upstairs in the bedroom she lay down on the bed, curled up and pulled the bedspread tightly around her body.

She lay naked on her back on a beach. The universe was black. Blacker than black — where she was there had never been light. The rough sand was scalding hot under her back, burning and scratching her skin. Yet cold water sloshed around her body. A wild sea roared beyond and the sound was deafening. Her eyes ached, staring wide open into space that was completely void of light, trying to make out shapes in a solid blackness. All around her the thunder of the sea. The air was thick and salty, sticking on her tongue and in her nostrils. She wanted to get up, to run, but the weight of the black night pressed her body deeper into the hot sand, paralysing her. Then, in the split-second between sleep and wake, there was a blinding flash of light and she could make out a wave of gigantic proportions, filling the entire universe and moving towards her, rising ever higher, gaining momentum, looming above in its deadly, shimmering enormousness, poised to break. Her hands clawed at the sand, breaking her nails. Soundless screams filled her mouth, choking her. When darkness swallowed her again, she knew the wave was breaking.

She only just managed to make it downstairs to the bathroom before she threw up. She shivered and her teeth chattered, yet her skin was on fire. She turned on the tap and let the cold water run over her hands, then put the wet palms against her cheeks. She cupped her hands and filled them, and drank. The house was dark.

Then it was not night, but not daylight either. She was in her bed, her throat throbbing. The sheets were twisted and rumpled. Colourless light filtered in through the half-pulled blind. She was desperately thirsty, but the door and the stairs were impossibly distant. There was a sick smell in the room. And such sad light. She closed her eyes.

She was on a New Zealand west coast beach, her bare feet on the hot dark sand. High hills loomed behind; in front of her the sea stretched to the horizon, thundering waves crashing onto the empty beach. She was panting, running, her feet sinking into the sand. He was ahead — all she could see was his bare back and his legs moving swiftly, his feet light on the sand. She was trying to catch up, struggling to fit her feet into his footsteps. But his strides were much longer than hers and she had to jump to reach each mark in the sand. She knew she had to hurry — the marks were getting fainter and more and more difficult to distinguish. The tide was coming in, moving closer and closer to the fading imprints in the sand. She stumbled, lost momentum and began to miss steps. When she looked up she couldn't see him any longer; she was alone on the deserted beach. She stopped and the tide reached her feet, lapping against her ankles. Helpless, she watched it sweep over the sand and in one brief stroke erase the prints, leaving a flat mirror behind as it withdrew. She sank to her knees, overcome by a sense of grief so intense it stopped her heart, her breath. Tears streamed down her face and she cupped her hands over her eyes. But her hands could not contain the tears: they fell between her fingers over her thighs until she sat in a pool of tepid water. When she lowered her hands she saw that the rising water was the brown, coppery stillness of a Swedish lake. She lay down and let the soft water carry her body, sinking deeper and deeper, the water closing over her face. Shafts of light filtered through the amber liquid, making golden flecks of innumerable drifting particles. She was gently rocked, weightless.

Then white morning light outside the window and she was back in her room. A blackbird sang outside the window. Veronika crawled out of bed and made it downstairs to the bathroom. She pulled off her nightgown and stepped into the shower, making no effort to wash, just allowing the water to run over her body. Eventually she sat down, her back against the tiled wall and her forehead against her knees, while the shower kept running. She sat immobile until the hot water slowly ran out, bearing the gradually colder water until the skin on her shoulders felt numb. She stood slowly, dried herself and returned upstairs, where she pulled off the crumpled sheets and replaced them with clean ones. The effort made her pant, and as she lay down the room seemed to pulsate with the beating of her heart. She closed her eyes.

Her father was standing outside a house. She didn't recognise it, but she felt that she ought to. He waved at her, smiling, and she wanted to wave back, but there were cars and buses obstructing her view, separating them. She stood on her toes, bending this way and that, craning her neck, trying to look over the traffic. But each time he came back into view he seemed to be further away. She tried to shout to him to stay put, to wait for her, but the noise of the vehicles drowned her words. She ran into the traffic, attempting to cross the road. There were buses, cars, trams and motorcycles all around her; she was caught in a turbulent sea of traffic. She realised that she would never reach the other side and she was overcome by a sense of loss that drowned all sounds. She stood like an island in the silent turmoil that swirled around her, unaffected and unconcerned.

There was a sound. Or was it in her dream? She was on her knees, on all fours, pounding her hand on the packed, black sand of the beach. She was trying to speak but tears kept choking her, and the more upset she became, the harder she beat, her palm burning. But then she was back in the bed, her hand stuck between the mattress and the edge of the bed-frame, and there was a knock on the door downstairs.

Except for the stale pancakes, the small jar and the blue thermos that were still on the table the following morning, it could have been the creation of a feverish brain. She had opened the door and her neighbour had been there, standing on the doorstep, peering hesitantly and looking distinctly uncomfortable. After a brief look and a nod, the woman's eyes had wandered, focusing on a spot just beyond Veronika's shoulder. And when she had spoken, it was with obvious effort, slowly and hesitantly. As if she were uncomfortable with the sound of her own voice and needed the time to listen to each uttered word before releasing another. She had said she would be right back. And then she had turned and hurried off.

Veronika had gone into the bathroom and looked at herself in the mirror above the hand-basin. Her face looked small, as if observed from a distance. She ran her hairbrush through her tangled hair and brushed her teeth slowly. She sat down on the closed toilet lid, her head between her knees, with her arms around her thighs. When she heard the front door open, she wrapped the dressing gown tightly around her body. She

22

lifted the sleeve to her face and buried her nose in the dark red terry cloth.

In the kitchen she saw that her neighbour had returned and was busy lighting the stove. She had her back to Veronika, and didn't indicate that she had noticed her. Veronika sat down at the table, watching the old woman. She was dressed in a large green woollen jumper and grey trousers, too long for her and clumsily rolled up to expose a glimpse of blue-veined pale skin between sock and trouser. She had found the frying pan and Veronika could smell melting butter. On the table was a small jar of jam and a dented old blue thermos. The old woman was frying pancakes and when she had finished the first one she brought the plate to the table. She opened the jar and spread a generous helping of jam over the pancake before rolling it up with a fork. Her eyes on Veronika's face, she pushed the plate across the table, but said nothing. Veronika took the rolled-up pancake between her fingers and took a small bite. It tasted wonderful — light, yet smothered in butter, and the jam sweet and filled with the flavour of wild strawberries.

The old woman returned to the stove, saying nothing, but every now and then she turned around, nodded and gestured with the spatula, urging Veronika to take another bite. Meanwhile she kept her focus on her task, pouring mixture into the pan, watching it set, with her hand on her hip holding the spatula, then turning the pancake with a swift movement before sliding it onto the serving plate. Still she said nothing.

She brought out two mugs and poured tea from the thermos. It was strong, almost black, and very sweet. Eventually she turned off the stove, rinsed the frying pan under the tap and sat down at the table. She didn't eat. Her right hand brushed the surface in front of her in quick nervous circles and her eyes kept drifting towards the window. After a while she stood up, took her jacket, which she had hung over a chair, and started to put it on. Halfway through, she stopped, turned to Veronika and said, 'Just open your bedroom window and call out if you need anything.' Then she pulled on the other sleeve and walked towards the hallway. With her hand on the door handle and without turning around she said, 'I will look out for you.' Then she stepped out onto the porch and softly closed the door behind her.

4

Put your hand in mine, if you so wish!

Three days were lost, a string of feverish phantom images all that remained. After the old woman left, Veronika went straight back to bed and slept until the following morning. When she woke, the stale pancakes and the blue thermos on the kitchen table were the only tangible proof of the visit. Her neighbour was an enigmatic apparition, interwoven with her dreams. She knew nothing about the woman who had appeared on her doorstep. But as she looked out the window, the house across the field no longer looked uninhabited.

She spent the rest of the week recovering, trying to write a little. But mostly she just sat at the table, looking out the window, her mind drifting. Then on the Saturday she dressed to go outside. Even the slightest task, like walking up the stairs to the bedroom, made her break out in a sweat. But the weather was mild and sunny and she decided she needed to get out, if only for a short walk. Also, she wanted to return the thermos and thank her neighbour.

She stepped out onto the porch and it was as if a whole season had passed in her absence. The bright sunshine made her squint as she walked across the field to the other house. The kitchen window was open, and when she knocked on the door she knew that her arrival must already have registered. Still, it took a while before the door opened. She was pleased that she had a specific reason for being there and held out the thermos as proof. The old woman stood well inside the door, only partly visible, her eyes squinting as she peered at her visitor. Veronika thanked her, commented on the jam. Mentioned the weather. The old woman said nothing, just nodded and took the thermos. Veronika kept up a strained one-sided conversation, but the words fell to her feet like dry leaves. Finally, she explained that she was off on her first walk since getting out of bed. She had no intention of asking the old woman to come with her, and was taken by surprise by her own words. 'Would you like to come with me?' The question hung in the air.

The old woman shook her head, but remained where she was, with the door half open. Veronika paused and looked out over the fields, overcome by a feeling of loneliness and an odd sense of disappointment. The quiet space between the two women lingered uncertainly. As Veronika turned her eyes back, her gaze was returned. The old woman seemed to pull herself up, a physical manifestation of her mind's decision. 'Wait,' she said. With a nod she indicated the unpainted bench fitted to the wall of the house along the porch, and disappeared, closing the door behind her. Veronika sat down in the shade. She heard the old woman's footsteps inside the house, then the sound as she closed the kitchen window. She came through the door wearing a threadbare cardigan over a checked man's shirt, corduroy trousers and a pair of black rubber boots with the tops cut off.

They set off down the hill, Astrid slightly stooped and with her hands clasped behind her back. Her boots made a hissing sound with each step. Suddenly Veronika thought of spring days as a child, walking outside in summer shoes for the first time after winter. Feeling so light she could fly. But here this old woman was awkwardly plodding along in heavy boots too big for her feet, stirring up little clouds of dust with every step on the dry road. Wild anemones dotted the bank on the southern side, the bright blue petals surprising signs of new life among blackened leaves and flax-coloured grass.

They walked down the hill, and when they turned into the main road at the bottom, they walked on the left side in single file, the old woman leading. Then they crossed the road and entered the path through the strip of forest. Here they could walk side by side again, and Veronika found herself falling into the rhythm of the other woman's steps.

'Are you all right?' Astrid asked, turning her head a little, but not stopping.

'Yes, thank you, I am fine,' Veronika replied, and they continued. There were no mosquitoes yet and they walked slowly. Veronika felt that the old woman might purposely have slowed her gait for her sake. It was cool in the shade under the dark firs, with an occasional shaft of light shooting across the path where the sun found a gap in the wall of trees. As they reached the other side of the small forest

27

they followed the path across the open fields. Suddenly the old woman stopped, her eyes focusing on a cluster of new buildings surrounded by struggling saplings. Veronika followed her gaze, reflecting on the strange choice of land for a housing development — on the muddy flat, fully exposed to the weather and with no view.

'My father used to grow flax here,' Astrid said, her eyes fixed on the group of brick buildings huddling together, braced against some unidentified threat. 'But then he sold it. My husband did. He sold the land to the council.' She stood silent for a moment, then turned abruptly and continued across the fields towards the river, her steps quicker than before. Veronika followed, a little out of breath. They walked along the riverbank for a while, looking for a good place for a rest. The river took a sharp turn and the bank scooped gently, creating a sheltered area, facing south and protected against the wind. Astrid took off her cardigan and spread it on the grass, and Veronika did the same with her fleece jacket. They both sat down and the old woman pulled off her boots, exposing pale bare feet with yellowing toenails. The sun was warm and the two women lay back, saying nothing.

Veronika stared up at the sky, where five seagulls drifted soundlessly. She thought nothing, allowed herself to doze. She started as Astrid gently tapped her arm, holding out a chocolate bar. Like Veronika, she kept her eyes on the sky. Veronika helped herself to a piece and closed her eyes again. The sun was warm against her face and she let her thoughts wander.

'My name is Astrid,' the old woman said. 'Astrid Mattson.' The words jolted Veronika back and she opened her eyes and turned her head. The old woman was still lying on her back, eyes closed now. Her hands were clasped on her stomach, as if in prayer. Or folded, after death. 'And you are Veronika.' She paused. 'There are no secrets here. Everybody knows everything about everybody. Or they would like to think they do. Secrets have to be well guarded, and the price is high.' She opened her eyes, squinting in the sun. 'Solitude. The price is solitude.'

The seagulls hovered above the water, sinking and rising like puppets on strings.

Astrid opened her eyes and turned her head, and for the first time Veronika noticed that her eyes were bright blue, cornflower blue. The effect was startling against the papery pale skin and wisps of grey hair.

Veronika sat up and hugged her shins, chin on her knees. She looked out over the river where the seagulls continued their intricate play.

'You mustn't misunderstand,' said Astrid. 'I am not after your secrets. I have no interest in other people's lives.'

She turned her head back and closed her eyes again. Veronika let her hand stroke the dry grass beside her and her fingers closed around a small stone. She lifted her arm and threw the flat pebble towards the water. It arched, disturbing the seagulls, causing them to lift with annoyed shrieks. The stone fell and broke the surface with a little splash.

'I have lived in this village my entire life,' the old woman said. 'And most of my life I have been alone.' Veronika looked at her face, but it gave no indication of her feelings. The eyes remained closed. 'I am old now. Nearly eighty years old. And with each passing day, it seems as if time goes ever more slowly. A day now seems longer than the entire life that went before. A season is an eternity.'

29

Veronika threw another pebble, missing the water and hitting a small bush on the bank. Her eyes were fixed on the slowly undulating surface of the river.

'And in this time without end, I have been alone in my house. Waiting. Guarding my secrets.' Astrid struggled to sit, rolling over on her side and pushing herself up with both hands. 'I have become good at keeping my secrets and I am an expert on solitude. But now . . .' Her sentence was left unfinished and they sat in silence.

'I used to come here with my mother,' Astrid suddenly said. 'We used to rest here on our way back from the lake. Strange, it is over seventy years ago, yet I can see her as clearly as I can see you. It is as if time is irrelevant. My life's memories take up space with no regard to when they happened, or to their actual time-span. The memories of brief incidents occupy almost all time, while years of my life have left no trace.' She looked at Veronika with a slight shrug of her shoulders and a hint of an embarrassed smile, her lips firmly closed and her cheeks blushing. 'I don't know why I am telling you this,' she said.

'I am scared of losing the memory of the most precious time in my life,' said Veronika, looking out over the river. 'Because it has happened to me before. I have no memories of my mother. I think now that perhaps I had to let them go in order to live. To remember her would have meant acknowledging the fact that she abandoned me. I don't think I could have lived with that.'

'I don't think I could have lived without those memories,' Astrid said.

Veronika stared at the old woman, her brows knitted. 'Yes,' she said after a pause. 'I am beginning to understand that I will have to remember. That I will have to hold on to every day. Take them out one by one, and make sure nothing is lost. But it is so very hard.'

'Let me tell you about my mother,' the old woman said. 'About a day that has stayed with me all these years, clearer in my memory than yesterday.'

5

*I shall build it with a towering turret
called solitude.*

Astrid

It was June, early summer and a day very much like today.
We had been down by the lake, just the two of us, walking
along the shore. Wading in the still icy-cold water, splashing
and jumping. Laughing. When my mother laughed, tears
streamed down her cheeks. It never ceased to disturb me,
though she would always notice and say, 'Oh, my little Astrid,
I am only laughing.' And she would wipe away her tears like
a child, rubbing both eyes with her fists. I never heard her
laugh in the house, only when we were away from home, just
the two of us.

That day, we ran along the edge of the water, chasing each
other. Laughing. A duck with its flock of little ducklings

watched from a safe distance. Eventually we sat down on the sand, panting. My mother wore a green skirt and the hem was soaked. She gathered the material in her hands, wringing out the water, exposing her white legs and bare feet. Her hair had come loose and fell over her shoulders and chest, and when she let go of the skirt she lifted her arms and pulled the hair away from her face, gathering it in her hands and piling it on her head. She sat very still, looking out over the lake. When she dropped her hands she pulled me towards her. Her hand stroked my hair and I looked up at her face. Her green eyes locked with mine for a moment before she pressed me to her chest. 'Remember this, my little Astrid,' she said. 'Always remember how the sun glitters on the water. How the mother duck cares for her babies. How blue the sky is. And how I love you.' And I knew with absolute certainty that there would be no more days like that.

On our way back we cycled past here. I sat behind her on the bicycle, my arms around her waist, pressed against her warm body. Her long copper hair blew around my face and I could feel the muscles in her back move with each push on the pedals. Our shoes were in the basket on the handlebars and she kept telling me to keep my feet wide, away from the wheel. 'Astrid, watch your feet!' she cried, turning her head to look quickly over her shoulder. The sky was absolutely clear; there was a smell of soil in the air from the potato fields either side of the road. It was such a happy day, but as I buried my nose into my mother's back I was fighting tears.

That afternoon she came downstairs, dressed to go out and with her hair tucked into her hat. In the kitchen she lifted me up, held me and pressed her face against my neck. I could feel her lips moving, but there was no sound. I looked out over her shoulder and saw the hoya on the windowsill, covered in clusters of velvety pink flowers. All these years I have kept a hoya in that spot in the kitchen window and each summer when the flowers open the perfume brings back that moment. I sat by the window, my nose pressed against the glass, and watched my mother climb into Mr Larsson's carriage. I kept watching as he whipped the horses and the carriage rolled off down the road. My mother never turned around to wave. It looked as if she was holding her gloved hands to her face.

They found her in a small hotel in Stockholm. She had cut her wrists and laid herself down by the window where there was no carpet. She had been lying there for three days. In the warm weather the blood had dried around her and they had to soak her skirt with water to get if off the floor. She was twenty-seven. I was six.

That evening, after my mother had left, I lay awake in my bed. It was still light outside, a pale summer night. The window was open and there was a breeze that made the cord of the roller-blind bounce against the windowsill. It was such a sad sound. Tap, tap, irregular and lonely. I lay on my stomach with my face pressed into the pillow and it was when I stuck my hands underneath that I felt the pendant. The little oval gold locket that my mother used to wear on a short chain around her neck. Inside, there was a lock of her hair. I sat in my bed, twisting the soft strands between my fingers, brushing them against my cheek, while the blind moved in the breeze. Tap, tap, tap against the window. I only found out what had happened to her many years later, but instinctively that night I knew that I had lost her for ever. I knew the moment she looked at me by the lake. I knew as I watched her come down the stairs. And I knew when she covered her face with her hands. I accepted the loneliness as a new state of life. Inevitable and permanent.

Perhaps that was when I became one with this house. It became my skin. My protector. It has heard all my secrets; it has seen everything.

I was an only child, like both my parents. After I lost my mother there was just the two of us, my father and I. There was a time when I longed for a family, for sisters and brothers, aunts and uncles, cousins. Now I am pleased there is nobody else. Just the house and me.

I am not sure whether my grandfather built the house with love, but I like to think so. I like to think he built the grandest house because he loved his only son. Because he wanted to give him the most beautiful view, the sweetest meadows with flowers, the fertile fields with flax and potato, the vast forests with trees to fell in the winter. I like to think there was love. I don't know what kind of man my grandfather was — he died before I was born. I don't know if it would have pained him to know what has become of his gift. To know that his son was not a farmer and had no love for the land. That money ran through his soft, slender hands like water, leaving only a dying house for the grandchild. To me, it seems right. It is all coming to an end.

When and where is the beginning? All these years while I have nurtured the memory of my mother, I think I made that moment the beginning and the end. Watching her climbing into the carriage, her back to me. It seemed to mark the end of all that was good, of life itself. And the beginning of a life-long solitude. Thinking about it now, I wonder. I think that perhaps there are no such defining moments at all. Beginnings and ends are fluid, long chains of events where some links seem so insignificant and others so very momentous, while in fact all have the same weight. What may appear as a single dramatic moment is just a link between what was before and what comes after.

6

The ache seeks company
The pain does not like solitude

Astrid stopped talking as abruptly as she had started, and they stayed like that, Astrid on her back with her eyes closed, Veronika hugging her shins looking out over the river. She couldn't be sure whether the old woman was awake — her hands rested folded together on her chest, lifting regularly with each breath. Finally, Veronika lay down, closed her eyes to the warm sun and dozed. She woke with a start to find Astrid standing by the river, her hands clasped behind her back and her eyes on the moving water. The sun had moved and they were in shade. Veronika stood up, shook her fleece jacket and pulled it on, and they started back. They walked in companionable silence, each left to her own thoughts. They took the main road, passing the shop. Veronika asked if Astrid needed anything, but the old woman shook her head and they continued up the hill.

It was after three when Veronika was back in her kitchen. She had expected to be exhausted, but instead felt strangely alert, as if her senses had been sharpened. She sat at the kitchen table all afternoon, reading and scribbling notes. She remained there while evening set in and the sun reluctantly withdrew in ever-extended rays of light, before finally dipping below the horizon. She had some cheese and crackers and a glass of wine. Still at the table, she rested her head on her arms and fell asleep, but woke with a start after a little while and went upstairs. She lay down on the bed fully dressed and closed her eyes. But her sleep was fretful and filled with elusive dreams. Eventually, she got up again and went downstairs. When she sat down at the table and looked out the window she noticed that there had been a subtle shift. The light had reached its most saturated grey and then turned, and the first birds had begun to sing. And with the return of the light she began to read again.

Each time she looked up, her eyes set on the other house. It stared back at her through the white morning mist.

Then, out of the corner of her eye, she saw a movement. In the bleak morning Astrid was slowly walking across the field. She trod cautiously, as if afraid of losing her footing. She wore the same clothes as the day before. Veronika didn't move, just sat and watched the slow progress until she heard the steps on the porch, followed by a hesitant knock. Two quiet taps, almost inaudible. And when Veronika opened the door, Astrid had already taken a step down, her body half turned away. She stopped in her tracks and slowly stepped back up onto the porch. She held her hands clasped over her stomach, twisting her fingers.

'I thought that perhaps you would like to come for coffee this afternoon,' she said, shifting her gaze from Veronika's face to the floorboards between them, then back again. 'I was thinking I might make waffles.' She paused. 'I suppose it's the same as pancakes.' She paused again. 'More or less.' She looked up, shrugged and smiled uncertainly. 'We used to have waffles for Marie Bebådelsedag, March 25. Annunciation Day. I don't know why, but people here always had waffles that day.' Another pause. 'I don't know why I came to think of that today. And you may have other things to do . . .' Her voice trailed off. 'Perhaps some other day.' She took a small step back, but Veronika stretched out her hand and held on to the old woman's wrist.

'I would love to,' she said.

'Three o'clock, then?' Astrid said, and when Veronika nodded the old woman turned and walked down the steps and back towards her house without looking back.

It was still early and Veronika suddenly felt tired. She went upstairs and lay down.

She was by herself in the swimming pool. She was wearing the orange plastic inflatable cushions on her arms and she hung upright in the water with only her head above the surface and her arms outstretched on either side. The tips of her toes only just touched the blue tiles at the bottom. It was dark and the water was illuminated by invisible lights along the edge, below the waterline. She could see her legs beneath, pale blue, like some underwater creatures with a life of their own. She could hear the voices of her parents, but she couldn't see them. Beyond the rippling bright blue water she could see nothing, only darkness. She knew they were arguing and she tried not to cry. There was a gust of wind and with a fright she realised she could no longer feel the tiles. She couldn't swim; she wasn't allowed in the pool on her own. She tried to run through the water, splashing as she waved her arms and gulping water as she tried to scream. Suddenly, a fierce gust of wind filled the air and it seemed to suck up all the water, pushing it to one end of the pool until it formed a large, blue, translucent wall at the far end, rising higher and higher. Then, just as it threatened to break over her head, she felt the tiles underneath the soles of her feet again. Soundlessly, the water sank back, embracing her and lifting her body until it was again bobbing gently on the surface of the illuminated pool, the tips of her toes back on the tiles. A tropical new moon hung in the sky and she could no longer hear her parents, just the cicadas playing loudly in the darkness. She knew her mother wasn't there any more. Just her father, in the rattan chair, smoking and staring into space. And she knew it was all her fault.

She woke with a start, disoriented, her mouth dry. It was after two and it had started to rain, a thin drizzle that fell straight from the white sky. She had a quick shower and dressed. On her way out she stopped on the porch, struck by the thought that she ought to take something with her on this first visit to her neighbour. She walked back upstairs and opened the wardrobe where she kept her bags. She had brought a few copies of her first book, *Single, one way, no luggage,* and they were still in a box with things she hadn't yet unpacked. She took one and weighed it in her hand for a moment, hesitating. Then she stood and went downstairs again.

She found a pen in the kitchen and opened the book on the table. 'To Astrid, my neighbour,' she wrote, then underneath, her signature. She turned the page and looked at the first paragraph. *The small rowing boat tipped to the side as he pushed it afloat and stepped inside. We were on our way.* She remembered the awe at the undertaking. Moving from the small streams and ponds of poetry and short stories into the ocean of a novel. Yet, even when the wind had sometimes died, or storms had hit, she had been confident of reaching her goal. There had been excitement, even joy. Frustrations, too, but of a creative kind. As she held the slim volume in her hand, she could recall the entire process. But it had nothing to do with where she was now, or the person she had become. She closed the book and left the house.

She could smell the waffles before Astrid opened her door. In the kitchen the old woman was busy by the wood stove, turning the waffle iron and checking the fire. A shiny, stiff white linen tablecloth covered the table, which was set for two with exquisite rose-patterned china. A delicate silver spoon and fork sat beside each cup and saucer, a folded linen napkin on each plate. Three candles flickered in a silver candlestick. The contrast with the rest of the room was striking: the faded curtains, the worn wooden chairs and the bare floorboards. Veronika felt moved, overcome by a sense of being treated to a ceremonial offering.

Astrid closed the oven door and brought the serving plate with the waffles to the table. They sat down, facing each other, neither taking the initiative to start.

'It was my mother's, the china set,' Astrid finally said, picking up her cup. 'I found it in the storeroom after my father died. He must have had it packed away when my mother died. I have never used it. I kept it in its boxes and only occasionally let myself handle any of the pieces.' Astrid's finger ran along the delicate ear of the cup. 'When you hold it up against the light it is almost translucent. As thin as an eggshell.'

Astrid pushed the serving plate towards Veronika and handed her the bowl with jam, and Veronika helped herself to a waffle while Astrid poured coffee.

'I brought you this,' Veronika said, and pushed her book across the table. 'Perhaps I feel a little like that about my book. That it is fragile and mustn't be treated carelessly.' Astrid ran her hand over the cover, left her palm on it, but made no attempt to open the book.

'It feels like such a long time since I wrote it,' Veronika continued. 'Perhaps it is a little like having a child. It is of you, but it is not you. Once it is born it has its own life. You are there to protect it and look after it, you suffer with it and rejoice with it. But in the end you have to let it live its own life. Step back and let it free. And hope that it will fare well.'

Astrid looked intently at her, as if she were digesting Veronika's words. 'Yes,' she said. 'We must let go of even the most precious things.' Her hand still lay on the book. 'What is the use of keeping them in boxes?' The look in her eyes became distant. Her lips moved, but Veronika couldn't catch the words. The old woman took the book from the table. She opened it and read the dedication, tracing the words with her index finger. She looked up as Veronika started to speak.

'I think I wrote this book because I wanted to try to understand the process of travel. The reasons for travel. How journeys affect those who travel. What separates those who do from those who don't.' Veronika looked out the window. 'I have travelled almost all my life. My father is a diplomat and after my mother left us he took postings overseas. In order to be able to provide better for me, I think. Here in Sweden, it would have been harder. I was looked after by nannies — amahs, ayahs, au pairs. But I travelled with my father.'

Astrid rose and walked over to the stove, returning to offer Veronika a top-up of coffee. She sat down again and leaned back in her chair, resting her hands on her lap.

'I look at my mother's cups today, and I think about all those years. I imagine that they were bought and given with love, unpacked here in anticipation. Gently placed in the cupboards. Then stored away, never to be used. Such a waste.' She looked up and Veronika was taken aback when she saw that the old woman's eyes were brimming with tears. As if embarrassed, Astrid stood up and walked over to the stove again, busying herself with the fire, adding firewood and watching it catch before closing the oven door again.

'Waste,' she said, keeping her back to Veronika. 'Such terrible waste. But then, in the wrong hands delicate things are destroyed. In the wrong hands a book can be just paper. To be used to light a fire or clean the windows. China as delicate as eggshells . . .' She paused while she closed the window over the kitchen sink. 'At least this way, it is still here. Perhaps one day, someone will unpack it again, as lovingly as my mother did. And allow it to be used as it was always intended.'

She returned to her chair, sat down and again took up the book.

'All those years,' she said, 'here in this house.' She looked up at Veronika. 'I have only left this village once. Once in a very long life. Yet I had so much to leave. So very little to stay for.'

7

Alone beneath the firmament
meanders the path that I walk.

Astrid
I used to dream about the world. It wasn't so much that I
dreamed of leaving, but I would sit here in the kitchen looking
out through this window. The village below was another
world, and beyond the fields and mountains lay yet others. I
would watch the river flow so eagerly on its way and wonder
where it was headed.

It was January, bitterly cold, the day I left to go and stay
with my grandfather, my mother's father. The school was
closed, the teacher was ill, and many of the children as well. I
have tried to understand why my father made the arrangement
for me to go. Perhaps he was afraid for himself. Or perhaps for
me. Not me personally, but the representation of me that

constituted his link to the future. Several of the children at school died that winter.

I knew that my grandfather lived in Stockholm, but there had been no contact with my mother's family since my mother's death. I had no memories of my grandparents, but I knew my grandmother had died not long after my mother did. My grandfather was just a faceless name. I knew that Stockholm was the capital of Sweden, but I had no concept of what the city might be like. It, too, was just a name.

Children have to build their world from such incomplete information. Other people make decisions for them, and only fragments of the rationale are ever conveyed. As children we inhabit a world built of incoherent snippets. The process of embellishing and filling the holes is an unconscious one, I think. And perhaps it continues all our lives. For me, being sent to Stockholm accompanied by Anna, the young girl who helped out at home, was totally incomprehensible, frightening. Yet once the decision was made I accepted it without question. 'It's just for a short time. You'll enjoy it, you'll see,' Anna said. And I travelled further into my loneliness.

When we arrived in Stockholm, the sight of the solitary tall figure on the platform held no comfort. Anna accepted a folded ten-kronor bill from my grandfather's gloved hand, and slunk away to the opposite platform with quick little steps. Without bending down, my grandfather looked at me and it was as if we were the only two people in the whole world. I stared back into his narrow face, but neither his eyes nor his mouth spoke to me. The grey beard had frost forming along the lower lip and in the moustache. He said nothing, just took my suitcase and led the way across the platform and out into the glassy winter afternoon. He had a large apartment in Drottninggatan and we walked there in silence. I had never seen large stone buildings before, never seen trams, paved streets or streetlights. But he gave me no introduction and I had to struggle to keep up with his pace. He was tall, and his long black coat flapped around his legs, making swooshing sounds. I hurried along, drawing quick, shallow breaths of the cold air.

There was an elevator in the building, and when he closed the gate behind us and we stood very close, but without touching, as the small carriage slowly creaked its way upwards I started to cry. When finally the lift stopped and we got out, and before he opened the front door of the apartment, my grandfather pulled out a monogrammed handkerchief, which he gave me without a word.

The apartment was large, with high ceilings and dark corridors that twisted and turned and opened onto dimly lit rooms. I could still hear the sounds from the street below, unfamiliar sounds. City sounds. A large woman with an apron came out into the hallway and took my grandfather's hat and coat, before turning her attention to me. She squatted and her face came level with mine. She unbuttoned my coat and untied the ribbons of my hat. 'So, this is little Astrid,' she said. Her light blue eyes seemed enormous as they searched my face from behind thick glasses. She stretched out her hand and lifted my chin with a light touch. She smelled like soap. 'I am Mrs Asp. Come, let me show you your room.' She walked ahead of me, down the corridor, with my suitcase in her hand. The black skirt stretched over her buttocks and she moved like water swelling to and fro, the ends of the apron ties swinging slowly. Her hair was grey and curly and collected in a loose bun at the nape of her neck. I thought she looked very old, perhaps as old as my grandfather.

I am not sure how long I stayed in Stockholm. Six weeks? Two months? The first evening I lay in my bed, watching the lights from the street on the ceiling. The bed was cold, and the weight of the dark red quilt pinned me between the starched sheets. I could hear faint music from another room. Nobody had made an effort to comfort me — explain why I was there, when I would return home. For me, it could just as well have been a permanent arrangement. Perhaps my father had simply sent me to stay in this place for ever.

I saw little of my grandfather. Left to myself, I wandered the shiny, creaky parquet, hands on my back. I was ten years old and I had to make an existence out of a solitary twilight world that had no beginning and no end.

Two things occupied most of my time: the library, and the piano. My grandfather's library smelled of dry paper and silence, and the walls were covered with books behind glass doors. Entire rows were dedicated to books with incomprehensible titles, written in letters I didn't recognise. The doors were locked, but there would be books on the desk by the window and on the small table beside the chair. I would sit on the edge of the seat and slowly turn the pages of a book, making sure I kept one finger where it had originally been opened. There were framed photographs on the desk and on the walls, most of them of my mother and some of my grandmother. There was a large portrait of my mother in a silver frame at the centre of the desk. Her body was half turned away from the camera and she was looking over her shoulder, smiling straight at me. Her hair was gathered and held back with a clasp, but fell freely over her back. She looked very happy. I would take the picture in my hands, holding it so close to my face that my nose almost touched the glass, and look into her eyes.

There were other photos of her, smaller ones. My mother in the saddle of a horse. With her graduation hat, arms full of flowers. In front of an easel, wearing a painter's smock and holding a brush. Arm in arm with her parents, all three smiling from underneath wide-brimmed sunhats. But there were no pictures of her with me. Or with my father.

The piano was in the sitting room. Mrs Asp kept it dusted and polished, but I never heard anybody play. I would go and sit on the stool and let my fingers play imaginary songs on the lid. One day I looked up and my grandfather was standing in the doorway looking at me. I froze, but he said nothing, just turned and walked away.

Occasionally, Mrs Asp would take me shopping. We would go to the market and buy fish. Or to the butcher.

'I wish I could buy pork. What's pea soup without ham?' she sighed one day.

'Why can't we buy pork?' I asked.

'Oh, well . . . we just can't,' she said. 'Your grandfather won't have it.'

One day we took the tram to the Royal Palace and the Old Town and watched the changing of the guard. It was very cold and when we got home Mrs Asp had me sit with my feet in a small washbasin with warm water while she made me hot chocolate. Mrs Asp had Saturdays off and I began to dread them. On Fridays she cooked soup and left it in the pantry for Saturday dinner. My grandfather would go out in the morning, leaving me behind. I spent most days in the apartment, but Saturdays were the loneliest. I never heard from my father, and slowly the village and the house faded from my mind.

One day as I was getting ready to go to bed, I heard Mrs Asp and my grandfather talking in the hallway.

'She spends every day here on her own. It isn't right. She's a good child, and it isn't right,' Mrs Asp said.

There was a long pause, before I heard my grandfather's voice. 'I never asked to have her here. She is the image of her father and it pains me to look at her.'

'She is just a little girl,' Mrs Asp said. 'Your grandchild.'

I couldn't hear my grandfather's answer, just the soft thud as the door to his study closed.

The day I left it rained. Mrs Asp walked me to the station. The snow had thawed, almost overnight, and large sheets of ice were falling from roofs. There were boards warning pedestrians to keep away from the pavement and in places it was cordoned off, forcing us to step into the street where dirty water ran in rivulets. At the station Mrs Asp came with me into the carriage and set my suitcase down in the luggage compartment. She bent over and hugged me, and the cold rims of her glasses cut into my cheek as she pressed her face against mine.

'Goodbye, my dear child. Don't think that your grandfather doesn't love you. Don't ever think that. It is just that . . .' She straightened, opened her shopping bag and pulled out a paper bag. 'Here, a little something for you to eat on the way,' she said.

She stroked my cheek with her cold hand, then pulled on her glove, closed her bag and stepped off the train. She gave a quick wave before turning, and I watched her disappear in the crowd.

Afterwards, I sometimes wondered if it had really happened. I had no mementos, no witnesses. Nobody to share my memories with. And when I looked at myself in the mirror in the bathroom at home I was surprised to find that I looked the same. Nothing had changed in the house, or in the village. I slotted back in. Unquestioningly.

I have never left this village again. You may find it hard to believe, but I have never even been to Borlänge. Or Falun, or Leksand. I have no idea what worlds lie beyond the forests and the mountains. Or where the river flows.

8

Come, sit by me, and I shall tell you all my sorrows;
we shall talk to each other about secrets.

Veronika carefully returned her cup to the table, suddenly concerned about the safety of the fine china in her hands. Astrid's cup sat on the table in front of her and she held both her hands around it, as if protecting it. She looked up.

'Let me show you my house,' she said. She stood and beckoned Veronika to follow. She crossed the spacious kitchen and continued out into the hallway, with Veronika following. 'I live in there,' Astrid said with a nod over her shoulder. 'In the kitchen, and the small room beyond. I don't even bother to heat the living room and I rarely go upstairs.' She pointed towards the closed door at the end of the hallway. 'That's the living room over there.' A wide staircase that turned halfway led to the second storey. Astrid paused on the first step and pointed to the closed door to the left. 'My father used to have his study in that room. Now I just use it for storage.' She continued up the stairs. At the top there was a large square landing with generous windows in two directions, four doors facing them opposite the top of the stairs, and one door immediately to the right. Veronika could see her own house through the window to the left and the road leading to the slope down the hill on the other side. A large weaving loom took up a good part of the space; a couple of wicker chairs and a small table stood by the window to the right. The most striking feature of the space was a number of rag rugs that crisscrossed the floor. Still more lay rolled up beside the loom.

'When my father died, I cut up all his clothes and started to weave. When my husband was taken to the rest-home, I began on his.' Astrid stepped onto one of the rugs and let the sole of her foot rub against it. 'It gives me pleasure to walk on them,' she said. She took Veronika's hand and led her to one of the doors in front of them. 'This used to be my room,' she said, and opened the door. The air inside was still and dark; a blind was pulled over the window. 'Later, when I was married, my father used it as his bedroom. He died in here.' Astrid's eyes swept over the narrow bed, covered with a white crocheted bedspread. 'When I found him he was already dead. Curled up, with his eyes wide open. I closed them and covered his face.'

She turned and closed the door behind her. 'This here is another bedroom,' she said, but didn't stop to open the door. 'A guest room, I suppose you could call it, although there have been no guests for such a long time.' She nodded towards the next door, told Veronika it was the bathroom, then walked across the landing. With her hand on the doorhandle of the fourth room she paused. 'The room over there is just a small bedroom. I . . .' She didn't finish the sentence, just nodded in the direction of the room to the far right, her eyes on her hand. Then she opened the door in front of her.

'This is the master bedroom,' she said, and stood aside for Veronika to enter. A large double bed took up most of the space, and a small writing desk with a chair stood against the opposite wall, beside a large free-standing wardrobe. All the furniture was old, the wood dark. The air was cool and Veronika couldn't pick up any smell. The impression was a little like a museum, a display of a distant past.

'I air the rooms once a week, but otherwise I never come upstairs.' Astrid walked through the room and opened the double doors to a balcony that ran the length of the house. Both women stepped outside and stood leaning on the bannister, looking out over the apple trees, still bare, across the fields, where the grass was still last year's, dry and flat, and down over the village and the distant hills beyond. The air was chilly and a light fog was rising from the valley below, like softly rippling grey gauze. 'Such a beautiful view. But, you know, it has never given me the slightest pleasure.' Astrid turned and walked inside. She waited for Veronika to follow, then closed the doors.

Later, as Veronika walked back to her own house, she took a deep breath. Although the new grass had only just begun to penetrate last year's dead groundcover, and the birch leaves still had a week or two to open, she could smell the budding growth. The days extended long into the evening now.

It was the week before Pentecost. Veronika wrote the note while she had morning coffee and put the envelope in Astrid's mailbox when she walked past. Afterwards, it struck her that perhaps the old woman wouldn't often check her box. She decided to give it a day or two. During the last few weeks she had seen Astrid outside, hard at work most days, weeding and clearing a small patch on the southern side of the house. Veronika hadn't tried to approach her neighbour, but had gone about her own life, taking her daily walks and writing most afternoons and long into the light evenings.

She checked Astrid's mailbox the following morning. The note was gone. Yet she didn't hear from her that day. Nor did she see her at work in her garden. But the window was open when she walked past and she thought the old woman was inside, watching. Suddenly, Veronika was able to see how beautiful the house and the garden must once have been: large birch trees in the front, their buds now pale purple and ready to burst, and the wide slope down towards the village at the back. Several large bird cherry trees stood on the western side, and beneath them an unkempt old lilac hedge. Veronika could imagine how beautiful it would look in a couple of weeks' time when the blossoms had opened. Along the back there was a small overgrown orchard with old apple trees, their trunks covered in grey lichen and with sporadic buds sprouting on bare branches. There must have been flowerbeds along the fence once — she noticed a few struggling daffodils among the weeds. It struck her that her own garden needed work. Her own garden? It wasn't her house, or her garden. She still had moments when she was overcome by a sense of surprise at being there at all. In the village. In the house.

She spent time going through her journal, rereading notes and adding new ones. Each time she would be instantly transported to another world, curiously more present and alive with each passing day, as if time and distance functioned as a magnifier.

She dreamt of the beach and the sea every night, but most mornings only a fragment would remain when she was fully awake. Still, the memory of the feeling lingered all day.

It struck her that her memories seemed clear, alive, here in this unrelated environment. She watched her neighbour's neglected garden slowly regaining life and preparing for summer, and the flax and budding pohutukawa of New Zealand intruded. Perhaps she had needed to get this far away in order to see clearly. To enable the memories to surface. But, although she was now beginning to touch the past, she wasn't able to turn it into words. She would spend hours on the computer with nothing to show. The book she had set out to write seemed increasingly elusive. On the one hand, there were the invasive memories. On the other hand, everyday life in the village. And then the book. Somehow she lived with all three, but there seemed to be no connections between them.

The following day she received the note. It was in her mailbox in the morning, although she hadn't seen Astrid deliver it. The envelope was yellowed and the glue dried out. The handwriting was elegant, but somehow gave the impression that the process of writing had been painful, a struggle with pen and words. But it was an acceptance.

'Thank you, dear Veronika. I was intrigued to get your note. There is rarely anything in my mailbox and I often don't bother to check. Imagine my delight at a personal letter. An invitation. Of course I accept. With all my heart.'

Astrid was coming to dinner.

9

Tonight, nothing, nothing has occurred, but something yet takes place.

Veronika had decided against meat in the end. It had been such a summery week, more suited to something light. She drove to the neighbouring village and bought three hot-smoked trout from the small smokehouse by the river. The first bags of new potatoes had arrived in the shop the day before, imported and overpriced, but she bought some.

It was all set. She had decided they would eat in the kitchen, by the window that was open to the light, early summer evening. Air wafted in filled with the smells and sounds of the approaching night: flowers folding, dew settling on the grass, insects of the day falling silent and those of the night stirring. The warmth of the kitchen added smells of wilting dill on steaming potatoes, sliced lemon, pungent cheese.

She had opened a bottle of New Zealand chardonnay and poured herself a glass. She stood by the window, waiting, and she raised the glass to her lips and took a first sip, letting the familiar flavours linger on her tongue. Apple, grapefruit, pineapple, feijoa, butter, grass — even experts struggled to find words to describe it. She looked out over the landscape, still wrapped in sunshine but distinctly evening quiet, and took in the immense stillness. She pulled the window to, leaving only a small chink. A fine film of steam covered the glass, the condensation running like tears. She was playing a recording of Lars Erik Larsson's *Förklädd Gud, God in disguise*. It was as if all her senses had come together to form a complete whole. The stillness of the evening, the smells from the stove, the taste of the wine, the sound of the music. She was surprised to realise that she was filled with a quiet, measured feeling of anticipation.

She put the glass on the table and went to the bench to prepare the mayonnaise. She started whisking oil into mustard and egg yolks in a bowl, her hip against the edge of the bench and one foot lightly resting on top of the other. Her hands moved, the music played. There was no forewarning of the sudden flash of a memory, which hit her with an almost physical force. The two of them in his mother's kitchen, laughing. James making mayonnaise. For her, in another life. His tanned hands moving with grace, effortlessly, doing their job while he talked to her of wonderful things to come. Her own hands stopped moving, resting on the bench, whisk in hand.

Just then, she heard footsteps on the porch. She put down the whisk and went to open the door. Her guest was lit by the lamp in the hallway behind, and Veronika saw Astrid's pale face set off by a man's white shirt. Her guest held out both hands, one offering a bottle filled with a dark red liquid, the other two small glasses, upside down and held by their slim stems. Veronika took the gifts, then gently touched the old woman's elbow with hers and guided her inside, kicking the door closed with her foot.

In the kitchen, Astrid refused the chair and instead walked up to the window, where she stood with her hands on her back, her eyes set on her own house. Veronika couldn't make out the shape of her body underneath the shirt, which was too big and hung loosely over her buttocks. Like the checked shirt she had been wearing on their walk, this one reached to mid-thigh, and the sleeves were rolled up to expose surprisingly slender wrists. Veronika could see the scalp through strands of grey hair at the top of the old woman's head. Astrid had removed her shoes by the front door and her dark socks were a little too big as well, leaving an empty tip at the toes. The bottoms of the dark trousers looked wet from her walk across the dewy grass. Veronika offered her a glass of wine, which she accepted with a small start. She held the glass with both hands and drank slowly, her eyes closed. Neither of them spoke and in the stillness the music filled the room.

They sat down opposite each other at the table. The hot steam from the bowl of potatoes stirred in the light breeze from the window. The trout rested bright pink on a plate, surrounded by wedges of lemon, with the mayonnaise in a separate bowl alongside. There was knäckebröd, wedges of the large round crisp local rye bread in a small basket, butter, and cheese so mature it was crumbling. They began to eat. Veronika talked a little about New Zealand, about the book.

'I thought I was writing a love story this time. Now I am

not so sure,' she said. 'It is as if it has slipped out of my hands. Or off the screen of my laptop. I am beginning to think that perhaps there is another story intruding.'

The old woman listened, saying nothing and keeping her eyes on her plate. Whenever there was a moment of comfortable silence, the music expanded to fill the space. Suddenly, Astrid looked up.

'They talk about me, I know. In the village.' She smiled, a strange little grimace with firmly closed lips. 'I don't understand how they still find things to say. But they always have. Yet they don't know anything worth knowing.' She turned the glass in her hand. 'I am sure you have heard that they call me "the witch". I don't mind. Perhaps there is something to that,' she said, again with an odd smile, her eyes on the glass. 'Lately, I have felt that it would be a relief to tell the truth. Or my version of some truth.' Astrid looked up and her eyes met Veronika's. 'But then who should I tell?'

Veronika said nothing, turning her wine glass in her hand. They continued the meal in silence, pausing now and then with the cutlery on their plates and elbows resting on the table. Veronika opened a second bottle of wine. She went up to change the music, putting on a recording with songs with lyrics by Erik Axel Karlfeldt. She paused for a moment to listen to the words:

> She comes across the meadows at Sjugareby.
> She is a little maiden her skin the fairest hue,
> yes, like meadow saxifrage, like wild rose blossom . . .

She returned to the table and sat down. Across from her, Astrid's face glowed with new warmth. Suddenly Veronika thought she could see the young woman who had looked out the windows with such longing, curious about the worlds beyond the forests and the mountains. She searched the old face for traces of the long-lost beauty, for hope. She thought about how modern science could develop the adult face from a child's. How it was sometimes done in cases when children went missing. She tried to do the reverse, constructing the young face from the old one across the table.

She remembered how one day, just after she had arrived, she had been to the shop, and the woman at the checkout had talked about 'the witch', insisting on showing Veronika an old black-and-white postcard. The tattered picture had showed a pretty, young blonde girl dressed in the traditional costume, posing on a wooden fence, a shy smile on her face.

'It's her. Truly. Hard to believe, isn't it?' the woman had said gleefully.

But now Veronika didn't think it was hard to believe: it just required a certain perspective. The eyes were still beautiful, bright blue, but they looked at the world with an expression of caution and suspicion. Poor eyesight, or perhaps life itself, had set them in a permanent squint. The skin stretched tightly over her forehead, and with her thin grey hair pushed back, the shape of the cranium was disturbingly exposed, evoking simultaneously a baby's vulnerable softness and a death's skull. Veronika thought about the young girl's thick braids falling from the edge of the hat down over her chest. The straight nose, the white teeth. The smile. Here, in the flickering candlelight, the nose was long and narrow, and the shadows down either side of the mouth were deep recesses. The mouth was a thin line, hiding gums that seemed largely toothless. It was impossible to associate it with the young girl's hopeful smile. And perhaps there had never been much hope.

When the music ended, Astrid sat with both hands on the table, her half-filled glass between them. She was looking out the window. Very softly she began to sing. *Hon kommer utför ängarna vid Sjugareby ...* She closed her eyes and her voice picked up, became more confident. Veronika looked at the old woman, then closed her own eyes and listened. While Astrid's spoken words were slow and hesitant, the lyrics of the song flowed with clarity and beauty. She finished the last verse and they were both silent for a moment.

'I used to love singing,' said Astrid. 'My mother used to sing to me — songs with words I didn't understand. I just absorbed them, the way children do. Listened to her voice and memorised the sounds. Later, at school, I learnt the local songs. Like this one.' And she began to sing again.

> Limu, limu lima,
> Dear God let the sun shine
> over mountains so blue
> over maidens so small
> who wander the woods
> in summertime.

Later, Veronika made coffee and as she put cups on the table, Astrid got up and collected the bottle and the two small glasses she had brought. 'I haven't bothered to look for them for several years,' she suddenly said, indicating the bottle with a slight nod. 'The wild strawberries.' She sat down at the table again and picked up the corkscrew. 'I planted them behind my house over sixty years ago. I got them from the forest and people said it couldn't be done. That wild strawberries couldn't be transferred. But I cared for my patch and the plants thrived. Each year I would run out to clear it as soon as the soil thawed in the spring. And later, I collected the new offshoots and planted them in pots until they were strong enough to go back into the patch. I kept looking after it all summer. Picked the berries as they ripened. They were the sweetest — small and bright red with a perfume that stayed on your hands long after you had finished picking. I used to make jam and conserve. Cordial. And sometimes this liqueur.'

She peeled off the wax covering the cork, inserted the corkscrew and opened the bottle. She put her nose to the opening and smelled the contents before filling the two glasses with the deep red liquid.

'I didn't know I still had a bottle left. It's been so long. I didn't think there would be anything left behind the house, either. But when I checked the other day, I found it — my strawberry patch — overgrown and hidden under weeds, but still there.'

She lifted her glass and looked straight at Veronika. 'Like secrets,' she said. 'Like memories. You can make yourself believe that they have been erased. But they are there, if you look closely. If you have a wish to uncover them.'

Veronika took her glass and held it up to the light. The content was burgundy red, mysterious and evocative, like a witch's brew. She could smell the fragrance of the ripe berries as she held the glass to her nose. She closed her eyes, took a sip and let the sweetness fill her mouth.

They sat at the table with their glasses before them, drinking slowly while the music played. Astrid kept her eyes on her house across the field, where pale sheets of mist were moving over the grass.

'Wild strawberries,' she said, turning the thin stem of the glass in her hand.

10

I walk on sun, I stand in sun.
I know of nothing other than sun.

Astrid

There was a place in the forest, high up on the hills beyond
the village, where I used to go. You had to know it to find
it, there were no paths. A small clearing in the midst of the
dense forest, with soft, silvery grass and wild strawberries.
I happened on it when I was out looking for mushrooms in
the autumn, and after that it became my secret hideaway. It
was as if the dark firs around it stood guard — over the place
itself, and over me. I sometimes came for a whole day, spread
my blanket and lay down. I was alone in the world, and safe.

The year I was sixteen, summer was late. But the week after
midsummer it arrived abruptly, with day after day of still, hot
weather. I had no direction, no one had talked to me about

what to do after leaving school. I drifted aimlessly, usually heading for my secret place in the early morning and returning only when the sun sank below the firs and the entire space was slowly overtaken by shadow. Nobody missed me.

It was a shock to discover someone there one day. He was kneeling, picking berries and threading them onto a timothy straw. I stopped in my tracks, well inside the shade of the trees. Although I made no sound, he must have felt my presence, for he stood up, holding the straw in one hand, like a strand of bright red pearls. He smiled and opened the palms of both hands, as if apologising. As if acknowledging that he was intruding, and surrendering to the rightful owner.

I recognised him vaguely. I didn't know his name, but I knew he came from the next village. He was tall and he looked strong, like someone used to hard work on the land. His skin was freckled from exposure to the sun and his fair hair bleached almost white. He had the clearest grey eyes with streaks of amber. But that, I only discovered later. He smiled and I cautiously left the safety of the shade, stepping into the bright sunshine. Turning my back to him, I spread my blanket and sat down, pulling my skirt down over my legs and hugging my shins. He stood for a moment, then sat down on the grass just to one side of my blanket. He turned to me and held out the straw. I hesitated, but he nodded, smiled and stretched his hand further forward until it became impossible for me not to accept the offering. We said nothing while I slowly pulled the berries off the straw, one by one. I offered him one for each that I put in my mouth.

After that first day the longing for the safety of my secret place slowly grew into a longing to meet him. Or perhaps the place and the boy merged in my mind.

His name was Lars. He was a year older than me, seventeen. He had further to walk, from the next village, and until the harvest was over he had little free time. I could never be sure whether he would be there when I arrived. On my way through the forest I used to pass a large granite block where I would stop, draw my breath and close my fists with my thumbs inside, then close my eyes and whisper: 'Please, please, please let him be there today,' before continuing. If he wasn't, I felt it was because of something I had done wrong. That somehow I had to earn the right to such pleasure. And for me, the place itself was no longer enough.

One day when I arrived I found him sitting on the grass, his hands cupped around something I couldn't quite see. As I came closer I heard the smallest sound from inside his hands. When I sat beside him, he opened them a little and allowed me to peek inside. All I could see was a soft bundle of grey down.

'It's a little baby owl,' he said. 'I found it right here, on the grass. Must have fallen from its nest.' He raised his gaze and scanned the solid wall of dark trees. 'It shouldn't be out and about in broad daylight.' He looked into his hands. 'A fox might find it. Or a falcon.'

We sat silent, watching the small bird in his hands, our heads so close his hair touched mine.

'I don't think it's injured.' He gently stroked the downy head with his finger. 'Just scared.' He blew softly into his hands. 'Perhaps if I put it in the shade under one of the trees it might survive until the evening and its mother will find it.'

'Kill it.'

I sat with my arms pressed around my shins, my forehead on my knees and my eyes closed. 'Kill it now,' I said.

I knew he was watching me, but I kept my eyes closed.

'The mother will never find it. Kill it!' I could feel tears pounding behind my eyelids and I was fighting to keep them out of my voice. 'Kill it for me.'

After quite a while I heard him rise, then his steps on the grass. Only when the branches rustled as he passed through the wall of trees did I release my tears. I sat hunched, hugging my legs, and the sun was hot on my back. My tears wet the cotton print of my dress. It felt as if he was gone for a long time, and all the while I struggled to control my crying. When finally he returned, he was empty-handed. I was still sobbing as he sat down beside me and put his arm around my shoulders. He said nothing. The air was still, the sun was high in the sky and we were the only people in the world. The skin of his arm was warm against my neck and his hand hugged my shoulder. I looked at our feet on the grass in front of us, his strong and tanned, mine slender and white.

It is in the nature of things to change. Nothing can last beyond its given time. And I think that instinctively we know what that time is. What is it that makes us know when the summer turns? The smallest shift in the light? The slightest hint of chill in the morning air? A certain rustling of the leaves of the birches? That is how it is — suddenly, in the midst of the summer heat, you are overcome by a tightening of your heart. The realisation that it will all come to an end. And that brings a new intensity to everything: the colours, the smells, the feeling of sunshine on your arm.

As we sat beside each other that day, the sun hot on our backs, everything around us was still summer. Yet everything had just shifted.

We lay down close to each other, holding hands and looking up into the blue sky. He had picked the last strawberries for me — the sweetest, overripe ones — and the taste was still in my mouth. He turned to me and put his head on my shoulder. He whispered my name, and the sound filled the entire world. He put his hand on my cheek and I could smell the strawberries on his fingers. I pulled him towards me and held his face between my hands, looking into his eyes before I kissed his mouth. I felt as if all my senses were sharpened, as if my tears had washed me clean and I was able to see all that was good for the first time. The infinite sky above, the glistening grass underneath, the dark trees guarding us. Every secret detail of his young body. The chest where the skin was still milky white, and the sunburnt arms. The downy hair on his neck. When he opened my blouse and let his lips run over my breasts, I knew I was part of the goodness. That I was beautiful. That I was alive.

I also knew absolutely that it would not last.

The following weeks I came back most days, each time stopping again by the granite block, closing my fists. But he was never there. Still I kept coming, well into autumn. One day in September I sat on the dry grass, as usual with my arms around my legs, my eyes on the trees across the clearing. Suddenly, out of the corner of my eye, I caught a soft, soundless movement. I turned my head and thought I saw a grey shape sweeping through the air, disappearing between the dark trees. I thought of the little downy bird gently cupped in his strong, large farmer's hands, and I knew with certainty that he had found a safe place for it.

Later, I heard about the accident. He had fallen from the loft in the hay barn during harvest. Death had been instantaneous.

The following spring I went back for the plants. I knew they would live, despite what people said.

It's more than sixty years ago, but my plants are still alive. I don't know if the clearing in the forest is still there, or if there are still wild strawberries there. It may very well be that it's overgrown, that the forest has reclaimed it. My patch may be the only place those wild strawberries still grow.

I wish now that I had held on to the memories of that summer. Perhaps things would have turned out differently if I had. Instead, I allowed what had gone before and what came after to overshadow it. I should have cared for it, the way I cared for my strawberry patch. Allowed it to develop new growth, new fruit. But perhaps they are one and the same, the strawberry patch and the memories of that one summer. Finally retrieved.

11

The heart must grow from dreams,
or it is a wretched heart.

The music had finished and when Astrid stopped talking the room was silent. Veronika blew out the candle and they were enveloped in the nebulous light that belonged to neither night nor day.

'Time. I don't understand it,' Veronika said. 'I think I have never grasped the essence of time. Memories seem to surface in no particular order, with no time attached. Yesterday can seem as distant as last year.'

Astrid did not respond, but stretched out her hand to pick up her glass. She took a sip and looked at Veronika.

'Some of my clearest memories are of the briefest moments,' Veronika continued. 'I have years of life that have left no traces, and minutes that are so ingrained in my mind that I relive them every day.'

'Yes,' the old woman said slowly. 'I think I said the same that first day by the river. I remember looking at those new buildings. To me, they were mushrooms, surprisingly grown overnight. The flax fields of sixty years ago seemed more real to me.' She sipped the liqueur, closing her lips tightly around a mouthful before swallowing. 'Telling you about that summer has given it back to me.' She bent forward a little, her hands on the table in front of her. 'It was never lost, you see; I just refused to listen. And now . . .' Her voice trailed off.

Veronika shifted on her seat, put down her glass and rested her elbows on the table, her chin on her clasped hands.

'My life now consists of fragments', she said, 'where some are so blinding in their intensity that they make everything else indistinguishable. What shall I do with these glittering shards? There is no pattern; I can't make them fit. With each other, or with the whole that should be my life. It feels as if my existence was extinguished in a flash, and afterwards my universe became incomprehensible. Just shards and particles, which I carry with me wherever I go. They are sharp and they still hurt to touch. And they are so heavy. I know there is more — there are less intense fragments that I need to make it whole. I want to remember everything. But perhaps I need to give it more time. Allow myself some rest. Distance myself a little, to see if I can make out a pattern. And face the truth about what is really there.'

Astrid's face was a white mask and her hair a halo, Veronika's a wide triangle where the eyes were dark hollows, reflecting no light. The first stirring of the morning breeze rustled the trees outside the window.

'When I met James it was as if a new time began. As if all that had been my life until then abruptly came to an end,' Veronika said, looking out into the night. 'And everything I had known before faded away. I was instantly transported into a world with brighter colours, sharper sounds, more intense flavours and smells. And for a time I thought it was mine.'

12

No, not you, not I, now just the one
Tonight, tomorrow and in a thousand years.

Veronika

In hindsight it appears as if that is how it was from the very beginning. Of course, that cannot be true. My memory is playing tricks again. But he smiled at me across the bar, pushed a beer my way and the world shifted a little. Until then my life had been safe. I had lived in a slow, amicably indifferent world that allowed me time to consider my actions. And that was the kind of world for which I had a map. In James's world I was forever lost.

We met in London, at the pub in Hampstead where he worked. I went with Susanna, the Danish woman who owned the gallery where I worked, and three of her friends. I didn't know the other people, but they seemed nice enough. A young woman, a freelance art reviewer; her partner, an IT consultant; and the third, Brent, who was one of the artists whose work Susanna exhibited. All four knew one another well, and perhaps I felt a little left out. When it was my turn to buy a round, I was glad to have a reason to leave the table. I walked up to the bar and ordered our drinks.

Beside me a rather drunk man in a striped business suit started moving in. Before I had consciously registered that he was bothering me, the barman leaned across and put his hand on the other man's arm. 'Hey, she's my girlfriend. Back off, will you.' Which to my surprise, he did. That was how I met James. I sat down on one of the barstools and took a sip of my drink. I thanked him and he asked where I was from. When I said Sweden, he smiled and said, 'Ah, as far away from my home country as you can get. I'm from New Zealand. Auckland, New Zealand.' His soft vowels seemed to caress the words. He had reddish-blond curly hair and grey eyes, and his smile picked me up and carried me off to places I had never been before.

'I am too old for this,' he said.

'For what?'

'For my OE. My Overseas Experience. I am thirty-one. I should have got it out of the way ten years ago.'

He laughed, throwing his head back a little, then leaned across the bar and took both my hands in his. And that is how he began to tell me about himself. Or rather, about some factual aspects of his life. Not about the man that was him. That was for me to discover.

I suddenly remembered my friends and stood to collect the filled glasses. But before I turned, he placed his hand on my arm and asked if I could wait until he finished.

'I usually take a walk on the Heath after work.' He smiled again. 'It's as close to nature as I can get here.' I agreed.

I returned to our table and it was another hour or so before my friends left. Susanna turned at the door and gave me a little smile and a wave. The pub emptied gradually, and just after midnight he came out from behind the counter and we went outside. The day had been hot and sticky, with the nauseous still air of a big city not built for heat. The night was warm, like velvety tepid water, and we walked onto the Heath.

He told me he had been in London for a couple of months, after travelling from Auckland through South-east Asia, the Middle East, Greece and Italy. He was now working to save his passage home. He was a marine biologist with no prospects of a job in his line of expertise. He had left a poorly paid job on a fish farm in Tasmania to come to Europe. The future was uncertain, but he was on his way home. To New Zealand. I had only the vaguest idea of this land. The most far-flung country on earth. I had travelled almost all my life, but never been to New Zealand. When he talked about it there was an intensity in his voice, a warmth.

His name was James McFarland.

Nightly walks on the Heath, after his shift finished, became our regular way of meeting. I would come up to Hampstead from the gallery in Knightsbridge and spend the evening nursing a beer, watching him while he worked. Laughing at the sheer joy of seeing him, hearing him. It felt as if I had never laughed before. Never been happy before. Now it feels as if that was the laughing of my life. My quota.

He told me he had promised his mother he'd be back for Christmas, so I knew it would soon be over. My own plans were vague. I had been in London almost a year, not giving much thought to the future. I knew my publisher was hoping for a second book, and I had been writing a little. Meanwhile, the work in the gallery provided an income. Susanna was generous and had put no pressure on me to commit myself to the job long term. Like me, she seemed happy to take life one day at a time. I had moved out of Johan's apartment in Stockholm, but had left my books and my cat behind. I suppose I had liked to consider the possibility that I might return. Just not yet.

James was house-sitting a flat on the top floor of a five-storey building right on the Heath. The owners were overseas. The first time he took me there was on a wet Sunday afternoon in October. It was his day off, and we had been to the Jewish bakery in Golders Green to buy bagels. On our way back the skies opened. We stopped at the Spaniards Inn for a beer, hoping the rain might ease.

I don't think I have a good memory, generally. My mother certainly used to tell me my memory was unreliable, that I could never remember anything correctly. But every day of those first weeks, months, has its own space reserved in my brain. I can pull them out and look at them and the colours are as bright and the resolution as sharp as ever. The exact look of his face across the table. His hands on the beer glass. My feet dyed bluish-black from my wet shoes when we got back to the flat. The skin of his arms rubbing against my face as he towel-dried my hair. We made love in the narrow bed in the small bedroom he used. It was gentle, not the passionate drama you would expect from such love. Sweet. With open eyes. As if this was the past, the present and the future, all at the same time, and we could not afford to lose even the smallest detail.

Afterwards, he gave me his tattered red bathrobe, took me by the hand and led me into the kitchen. That was the first time I watched him cook. His hands as he expertly cracked eggs, chopped spring onions, sliced tomatoes. I could talk about his hands — give every finger time. Such good hands. Hands that would give my body such pleasure. Hands that handled food with such love, such instinctive love. Later, I would see them touch other people he cared about and animals. On the steering wheel of his car. But mostly I remember them on my body. Touching me.

I knew he was leaving. He had told me from the start. Yet as the moment approached, we avoided the subject. We never talked about anything outside the world that contained the two of us. There. Then. We spent all our free time together, going to movies, galleries, museums. We walked in parks where the trees and lawns were shedding life, preparing for winter. We ate in small restaurants, but more often at his flat. We made love. The world went on its way without us.

Then, inevitably, it was time.

'I've booked my ticket,' he said one day as we set out for our walk on the Heath. It was no longer warm, but we kept to our routine. He had his arm around my shoulders, looking straight ahead, not at me. We walked, and I tried to keep his pace, allowing my body to ride on his energy, half carried.

'My flight is three weeks from now,' he said. Three weeks. It was like being told the exact span of the rest of your life. Suddenly the smallest detail became distinct and utterly significant. He stopped abruptly and turned me towards him, holding my shoulders in a firm grip.

'I love you, Veronika.' He bent forward and kissed me, without pulling me towards him. I closed my eyes, and when

I opened them my gaze landed on the faces of two young girls, standing at a distance behind James, giggling excitedly. Somehow the look on their faces confirmed what he said.

That evening we sat on the floor in the dark living room, in front of the gas fire, side by side with our legs crossed in front of us. He turned towards me, got up onto his knees and pulled me up until we faced each other, knees touching.

'Come with me,' he said, holding both my hands. 'I've forgotten how to live without you. I can't remember how I used to get by. Please come with me, Veronika.'

I looked at his face, scanned every minute detail and stored the images. The fair skin stretching over his forehead, the reddish-blond hair rising from an intricate pattern of vertices. The small scar on his upper lip. The chipped front tooth. Had they happened at the same time, the lip and the tooth? I knew so little. And what I knew, I was already treating as history. Observing, recording, storing. I tried to imagine how he would age. What he would look like as an old man.

He turned away and lay on his back, his arms clasped under his head. I watched his profile, memorising every line.

'I lie awake after we have made love and watch you,' he said. 'I worry that you will quietly pull back the covers and slip away if I close my eyes. Slip away like a deer into the night.'

He stretched out a hand and pulled me towards him. We lay still. My eyes were closed and I filled my head with his smell. I could hear cars passing in the street below and their headlights painted drifting patterns on the ceiling. The gas fire hissed.

He left on a Saturday morning. We had agreed that I shouldn't come with him to the airport. We sat at the table drinking coffee. It was still dark outside.

'I have something for you, Veronika,' he said, and pushed a small parcel across the table. 'I want you to open it after I have left, and I want you to use it often.'

I held the parcel between my palms, struggling not to cry. 'I have nothing for you, James,' I said.

'Just give me a smile,' he said.

And it was the hardest gift to give.

13

Do not fear the darkness
for in it rests the light.

In the silence a blackbird started singing hesitantly. Astrid stood, leaning heavily on the table, her movements awkward, as if her joints were aching. She pushed the chair back, taking the time to make it a gentle, soundless process. She walked around the table, bent forward and took Veronika's face in her hands. Her palms on the young woman's cheeks, she looked at her intently for a moment.

'Love,' she whispered. 'Always remember your love.'

She dropped her hands and crossed the floor. Her feet made no sound. Veronika turned her head and her eyes followed the figure slowly making her way into the hallway. She looked at the feet with the too-large socks, the shirt wrinkled across the back. The thin hair on the back of Astrid's head. She loosened her clasped hands and let them drop to her lap, inhaling deeply, as if she had been holding her breath for a long time. She heard the front door open and close, and when she looked out the window she saw the old woman treading slowly through the grass, gradually merging with the lingering mist. And she put her hands to her face and cried.

Summer arrived abruptly, the week before midsummer. Veronika fitted mosquito nets over the windows so she could keep them open and create a breeze through the house. The birch trees went from sheer pale purple through shy green to full summer exuberance in a few days, and the delicate bluebells covered the meadows with a quivering brush of purple. The bird cherry trees blossomed and filled the air with perfume over a few intense days, then the petals fell like snow. When Veronika walked along the river she was passed by children on bikes on their way to the lake for a swim, towelling robes fluttering in the wind behind them and large rubber tyres across their shoulders. School had finished for the year; summer lay ahead, open-ended. She hadn't seen Astrid since the evening of the dinner. And when she passed her house the kitchen window was opened only a crack. She could see no life inside.

In the village the preparations for midsummer festivities were under way, carrying with them an atmosphere of warm anticipation. The open area along the river beyond the church had been mowed and stands erected on one side. When Veronika walked past the shop, people were lingering outside in the sun, chatting and smiling, their faces turned towards the sun.

Two days before Midsummer's Eve, Veronika walked across

and knocked on Astrid's front door. It was late afternoon and although the sun was still high in the sky a lazy drowsiness filled the air; birds and insects seemed to be resting. She knocked once and waited. Then again. She heard no sound. She tried the handle and the door opened. She stood on the threshold, waiting. 'Astrid?' she called, the sound tearing the still darkness inside. There was no response. Leaving the door open, she stepped inside. As her eyes adjusted she could see the hallway ahead, all doors closed. She stood still, her ears alert, but heard nothing. She walked up to the closed kitchen door and listened again before pressing down the handle.

The old woman sat at the table, her hands around a mug on the table. The curtains were drawn and the sun filtered through the faded print material, filling the room with a tired, ochre light. Veronika felt as if she had entered a dream, a surreal, staged scene.

Astrid gave no sign of having noticed the visitor — her eyes were fixed on the window. Veronika walked up to the table and sat down. She stroked the cracked oilcloth with her palm, and waited. Eventually she said, 'I am sorry to intrude like this, but I was worried. I haven't seen you for almost two weeks. Just the open window in the morning.' The old woman said nothing. 'And Friday is Midsummer's Eve. I was hoping you would come with me to the village and watch the raising of the maypole.' She looked at her neighbour, her words hanging in the air. Astrid remained silent, her eyes fixed on the window. A fly buzzed helplessly on the windowsill.

'He is dying,' she said, her eyes turning from the window and looking straight into Veronika's. 'My husband is dying.'

Veronika's stared back, uncomprehending.

'They rang from the rest-home.'

Astrid's fingers ran over the rim of the empty mug in front of her and her eyes returned to the window. 'He's been dying for such a long time. I have waited for so very long. But now they say it's imminent.'

Veronika stood up, put the kettle on and put two fresh mugs on a tray. 'Let's go outside,' she said, gently touching Astrid's elbow. Astrid slowly obliged, clearly preoccupied with her thoughts.

Before taking the tray outside, Veronika carried Astrid's folding chair to the back of the house and placed it near the wall in the light shade from the apple trees. She returned for the tray and Astrid followed her.

The wild strawberries were in full bloom, the white flowers like snowflakes on the grass. Veronika guided Astrid to the chair and sat down on the grass beside it. A large bumblebee wobbled over the flowers, as if dazed by the abundance. Veronika rested her back against the warm wood of the wall behind her. Astrid sat still, her eyes closed and the coffee mug in her hands.

'Such a long wait,' she said. 'A lifetime.'

14

Till hatred only you breathe . . .

Astrid

I have longed for this death since the day I was married. Sixty years. Now that it is here, I understand that it has no significance. That it was never about him. What I have thought started the day I was married actually began much earlier. The marriage was just the defining moment. It was the day I gave up my life.

It was June. I had willed the weather to remain grey and cold but the day turned out summery, with a fiercely blue, empty sky. The bells ringing. A grand ceremony. The priest came from Uppsala, the flowers from Stockholm. Lily of the valley, large and waxy with a sickly perfume. I wore the traditional costume, not the white dress my father had requested. The one thing I decided.

The evening before, I sat in my room with the box that held my mother's wedding dress. I opened the lid, lifted the dress gently and held it against my body. I put it to my face, closed my eyes and inhaled. But there was no smell: the dry silk rustled against my skin but it had nothing to say. I set the veil on my hair and sat naked on the chair in front of my mirror with the lace falling over my shoulders. I looked at my face, the pale oval with the blue eyes staring back at me. I traced my eyebrows with my index finger. Then the ridge of my nose. My lips. I held up my hands and looked at them, stroked the creamy skin on the undersides of my arms. I loosened my braids, combed my long hair with my fingers and let it fall down over my breasts and shoulders. My eyes took in every detail of my body. The exact colour of the skin. The pink nipples. The blonde pubic hair. I cupped my breasts, stroked my flat stomach, my thighs. I wanted to memorise it all before I let it die.

In the morning I dressed in my costume. The thick woollen skirt, the vest, the linen blouse, the apron, the shawl. The shoes with brass clasps and the red woollen stockings. I walked down the stairs in the heavy outfit and into the summery day, feeling colder than I had ever been before. Afterwards, people said that I wore the funeral version — the dark apron, no jewellery. It is not true. But I wore the costume instead of my mother's white dress, and it wasn't enough to warm me.

My husband married a farm. He married the land and the house. The fields with rye and potato and flax. The orchard and the meadows. The forests and the timber. And he married the family name. My father thought he had negotiated a future for himself and for the farm.

I married death.

The church was so full there were people standing at the

back. My father was hosting a large dinner afterwards, and guests had travelled from as far as Stockholm. Many had come just to look. I walked up the aisle with my father and my hand on his sleeve was numb. Even now, after all this time, I can see the face of the priest, his brown eyes locking with mine. He was an old man, overweight, and I could see that he was panting. There were drops of perspiration on his brow. But his eyes were kind. I set my eyes on his and willed them to stay there. I remember nothing else.

Afterwards I watched the backs of my father and my husband as they were signing the ledger. They looked like business partners, signing a successfully completed transaction.

I was eighteen years old.

I walked out onto the steps of the church, my arm resting on my husband's. Guests threw rice over our heads and I could see their smiling faces, their moving lips, but I heard no sounds.

We all returned home for the reception. My father had arranged for the barn to be cleared. The wide doors on either side were open, and the frames had been trimmed with branches of birch. Long tables were set up inside, covered with white tablecloths and decorated with wild flowers. A group of local fiddlers had been hired to play and as our carriage drove up the music began. Guests congregated, drinks were passed around, the fiddlers played, but to me it all swirled in a silent vortex. Deathly silent.

As we were asked to move inside and sit down to eat, my father took my hand, raised it and turned me slightly away from him. His eyes swept over my body before he bent forward and let his lips brush my ear. He said nothing, but the smell of brandy lingered around my head. He abruptly dropped my hand and we walked inside.

I sat at the bridal table all evening but I heard none of the speeches, tasted none of the food. Time had ceased to exist. When after dinner my husband stood, stretched out his hand and indicated the dance floor, I found it so extraordinary that I laughed. He took my dead body in his arms and awkwardly moved us around the floor, while a wall of sweating faces looked on. As soon as the guests joined the dancing, he released his hold on my waist, turned and left the floor. I stood for a moment while the throng of guests revolved around me. When I left the barn it was as if the swirling mass parted to grant me passage.

Outside, the white day had given in to a white night. There were no stars in the pale sky. I could hear laughter from behind the lilacs — a man's guttural bursts mingling with a woman's pealing giggle. I walked around the house and sat down on the grass by the strawberry patch. I lifted the apron to my face, but I had no tears.

Later, I lay in the bed upstairs in the master bedroom. My father had moved to the smaller bedroom on the other side of the landing and he had had the girl make up the big bed for us. Nothing had been changed from the time when my mother had lain in the bed. It was as if I could feel the outlines of her body, where my body fitted. I lay on my back, my hands folded on the white linen sheets over my chest. I twisted the plain gold wedding band on my finger and looked out the window. The bird cherry trees were covered in blossom and petals fell like snow in the light breeze. I could hear guests laughing in the garden.

The sun was over the horizon when I heard his steps on the stairs. He opened the door clumsily and I could hear him undressing, his shoes falling to the floor. I lay still, my eyes closed. The room filled with his exhalations, his smell, and I struggled to breathe. He fell into bed, his body hot next to mine. I sank deeper into the recess of the mattress.

He was such an insignificant man. The first time I met him he stood beside my father, a pale copy. Smaller, younger, yet somehow similar. He was short, and already balding at twenty-five. His eyes looked out on the world through thick glasses, without expression.

As he lay beside me in the strange no man's land of the June night, his eyes were closed. He rolled over and lay on top of me, pushing my icy body ever deeper into the mattress. His hands were on my skin, his breath in my ear, but my eyes were on the ceiling, following a crack from one corner across the entire white expanse. My body rested in my mother's.

When the sun reached the tree outside the window, I got up. I had to climb over his sleeping body. He was on his back. His face was empty, his eyes closed and his mouth half open, with a trickle of saliva running down his chin. I stood by the window looking out, but I saw nothing. Then behind me I heard him speak, his voice a hoarse whisper.

'It's all mine now, you know. Everything you can see through that window. All mine.' He cleared his throat loudly, coughing up phlegm. I turned to look at him.

'There is nothing here that belongs to you,' I said. 'Nothing.'

And so my long wait began.

15

It shall arrive, this moment,
This chilling minute . . .

'Now that the time has finally arrived, I am frightened.'
Astrid bent forward, arms crossed over her chest, her eyes
on the grass at her feet. 'I am so afraid.' Veronika watched
the bumblebee, still pursuing its solitary inspection of the
strawberry flowers.

'Would you like me to drive you there?' she said. Astrid
turned her face and looked at Veronika, but she said nothing.
'I'll come with you. Let me ring the home.' Veronika sat with
her legs stretched out in front of her, leaning back, her elbows
on the grass.

'I am not afraid of facing him,' Astrid said. 'I am afraid of
facing myself.' They sat in silence. Astrid leaned back in her
chair with her face towards the sky, eyes closed. When she

spoke again her words were slow, as if she were searching deep inside for them.

'Such a long wait. I allowed life to slip away while I nurtured my hatred inside this house. Now I realise I made it my prison. I told myself I was safe here. I told myself I had to wait for the house to become my own. I chained myself to the house. Now I can see that all these years I have waited to be released, when all the time, the only bonds were those I made myself.' She looked at Veronika and her eyes were filled with such grief that Veronika had to look away. 'And now the time has come. I must face the truth.'

Veronika did not respond, just reached up and placed her hand on Astrid's arm. The old woman had her eyes on the horizon, and when she spoke again she squinted, as if trying to focus on a point in the far distance.

'I know now that it didn't begin with my husband. It was inside me already when I married him.' She sat silent, her head resting against the chair back. 'It began here. It began in this house.'

16

The young king Lily of the Valley,
king Lily of the Valley white as snow,
he mourns his maiden lily
his Princess Lily of the Valley.

Astrid

I cannot remember that my father ever touched me. Not lovingly, not in anger. He was away for long periods and my only company was a succession of young girls who kept the house. When he was home he rarely came out of his study. He seldom spoke to me, and when he did it was usually in short sentences. Practical instructions, never personal. He never once mentioned my mother, and instinctively I knew not to. I don't think I ever saw him properly — as a man, as a person. Children never see their parents as people, I suppose. Only later, when I looked at photographs of my father, could I see what he looked like. Very fair, with a perfectly symmetrical oval face, soft mouth, straight nose. The striking feature was his eyes — very light blue, like ice, and almost transparent, as if lit from behind. On a woman it would have been a beautiful face, but on a man the features were disturbing. Too beautiful. I used to be told I looked like my father, but I have never seen the likeness. I have never thought of myself as beautiful, not even when perhaps I was.

He wasn't very tall and he was rather lightly built. His hands were very white, with long fingers. An academic's hands, not a farmer's. He was sent to Uppsala to university, but I don't think he ever completed a degree. In those days it was unheard of here for anybody to go to university. It set him apart, absolutely. But when my grandfather became ill, my father was called back to manage the farm.

He had met my mother at university, I think. I have tried to imagine what brought them together: this weak, slight man and my tall, striking, laughing mother. It is impossible for me to understand. But just as we are unable to see objectively how our parents look, I think we are incapable of imagining their life together. I only know that all that was good in my mother died here. I have no way of imagining my father's reaction. I remember only my own loneliness, my own grief. In my memory I am alone by the window as she leaves. Where was my father?

All his life, he wore his wedding band on his ring finger. On the other hand a gold signet ring on the little finger. In the evenings he used to sit in his armchair in the study, a glass of brandy in his hand, and the signet ring would make tinkling sounds as his finger tapped the glass.

I think it might have been easier if it had happened regularly.

As it was, after that first time I lived in permanent dread, my ears alert to the slightest sound or movement in the house. Only when I knew he was away could I breathe properly.

It was just after school had finished for the year. Early summer, the year I was thirteen. I was upstairs in my room. I had picked lily of the valley and I was arranging it in two small vases: one for my desk, one for the bedside table. It was as if I felt the sound before I heard it. As if a preceding cold breeze alerted me. Then, the sound. He called me. The single word shot through the quiet house like a flash of ball lightning. My father rarely spoke to me, and never used my name. But here it was: 'Astrid!' His voice was not loud, yet it was a deafening sound, tearing up the stairs and into my room. The flowers dropped from my fingers and scattered over the desk. In an instant, the world where little girls like me picked lily of the valley vanished. I was in new territory, where there were only the two of us.

My father was in his study when I came down the stairs. He had pulled the curtains. He sat in his chair, glass in hand. I stood on the doorstep, rigid, my arms tight against my sides, my hands hard fists. With a nod of his head he beckoned me into the room. I stood in front of him and he stared at me. His pale eyes shone; in the dim light they glowed as if alight. They stayed fixed and expressionless on my body as he opened his mouth and told me to undress.

My stiff fingers struggled with buttons and clasps, while his eyes remained set on me, unblinking. When I stood before him naked his eyes moved slowly over my body. There was no sound: all was silent in this new world. After an eternity he gestured for me to turn around. I stood with my back to him, my eyes on a partly burnt log in the fireplace in front of me. The only sound was the rhythmic rustling of wool against wool, his arm against his trousers. Time passed. My entire youth passed.

Only when I heard his steps across the floor and the sound of the door closing did I turn around. When I bent down to gather my clothes it felt as if my body would never again be able to move properly. My feet were numb, my legs stiff and I trod the stairs with difficulty. I walked slowly across the upstairs landing, carrying the bundle of clothes in my arms like a dead body. I locked myself in the bathroom and filled the hand-basin with cold water. I rubbed my entire body with a washcloth until the skin burnt. Then finally I cried. I sat on the floor, with the washcloth over my face, and cried until I had no more tears.

Later, when I lay in my bed, the room still smelled of lily of the valley. I lay absolutely still, on my back, arms crossed over my chest. For a moment I saw myself from a great distance, as if observed from above. I saw every small detail: how my hair was still neatly plaited, the pattern of the bedspread, the white desk where the flowers lay scattered. And I wanted to make it right again. I wanted to bring the girl in the bed back to the world before. But I couldn't. All I could do was to leave her where she was.

17

There is only absence here, sitting,
of a person departed long ago,
leaning lightly onto the armrests
surrounded by night.

Veronika was poised with her hand in the air ready to
knock when Astrid opened the door. She must have been
standing waiting. The old woman had made no effort
to make herself presentable: her trousers were the usual
baggy corduroys, the shirt the checked flannel, sleeves
rolled up.

When their eyes finally met over the roof of the car, Astrid's
were naked and wide open, gazing into Veronika's with an
expression of terror. Like a child's, hiding nothing. It was
just after nine when they left, and as they drove down the
unsealed road a cloud of dust rose behind them. Astrid sat

with her hands pressed between her knees, hunched, and staring straight ahead.

They drove in silence. There was more traffic than usual, because of the forthcoming long midsummer holiday. Veronika turned on the radio and tuned into the local station, which played light summer music. She kept the driver's window slightly rolled down and the sound of the air competed with the music. Neither of them spoke for the entire drive and Veronica wondered if Astrid might be asleep.

They turned off the main road and arrived at the rest-home just before ten, in time for the arranged meeting with the head nurse. The building was a drab 1970s construction: three low structures, painted dark green and joined together by glassed passageways. No water spurted from the funnels of the small concrete fountain that sat in the centre of a circular flowerbed where wispy rose bushes struggled in the parched soil.

They walked up the metal steps to the front door and went inside. The reception area was empty and the still air smelled of detergent and dying bodies, bland food and forced cheerfulness. The small counter to the right had a vase of drooping cornflowers, but the seat behind it was empty. When Veronika pressed the bell a woman emerged through the door behind. The rubber soles of her shoes squeaked as she crossed the shiny linoleum floor. She was middle-aged, with a plain face and a solid body that seemed to have been poured into her uniform, which stretched over her breasts and stomach. Her smile was professionally comforting as she extended her hand to greet them.

'I am Sister Britta,' she said.

Veronika looked at Astrid, who stood passively, her hands hanging straight down. For a brief moment the nurse's hand remained unacknowledged in the space separating the three women, before Veronika grasped it.

'And you must be the daughter,' Sister Britta continued.

Veronika gave Astrid a quick look, but the old woman remained immobile, her eyes vacant.

'No, no,' Veronika said. 'Just a friend.' She realised that the nurse had made a very plausible assumption. She was surprised to realise that she didn't mind.

They were led into a small office with a desk and two plastic chairs facing it. The nurse took her seat behind the desk and indicated to Veronika and Astrid to sit down. Sun streamed in between the slats in the blind covering the window behind the nurse, leaving her face dark and outlined by frizzy hair, as if tangled in cobwebs.

'Mr Mattson is dying,' she said. 'As I explained to Mrs Mattson on the phone, there is nothing more we can do for him. It's been a very long process, but now it is a matter of days, perhaps hours.' She clasped her hands on the desk in front of her. 'Now, Mrs Mattson hasn't been a frequent visitor . . .' Her voice trailed off. 'But as we are now talking about a very short time, a *very* short time, I thought she would appreciate the opportunity to say goodbye properly.'

Silence followed, and they could hear the sound of a toilet flushing and of metal clanking against metal.

The nurse nodded to herself, approvingly. Her clasped hands on the shiny surface lay still. Birds chirped, and a smell of freshly cut grass wafted in through the window. Outside, life went on; inside the small room, the presence of death was sucking up the air.

'Let me see him.'

The words were spoken quietly, yet they seemed to still all

other sounds. Even the birdsong seemed to pause momentarily. Astrid stood, supporting herself heavily on the back of the chair. 'I want to see him now.'

He was in a double room but the other bed was unoccupied. The room faced north, and despite the warm weather it seemed cold, the air still and stale. Nothing in the room looked private. The body in the bed was as lifeless as the plastic-covered chair in the corner by the window and the grey-striped curtains that hung listlessly either side of the window. They stood at the foot of the bed and looked down on the immobile shape that occupied it. Veronika could see no signs of life. The face was a white paper mask, stripped of personality. The eyes were closed. The body seemed so light it hardly dented the mattress or the pillow, and there were no creases in the white cotton blanket that was stretched firmly over the bed and tucked under the mattress. It was a human being reduced to a neutral physical form: limbs and organs, but no identity. It was impossible to envisage the man who had once inhabited the body.

'I have come to watch you die, Anders,' Astrid said to the still body. 'And I will be here until it is finished.' Were they words of comfort? Or a threat? Veronika looked at the old woman, but she found no clue in her pale face. Astrid's eyes rested impassively on the patient. She stood by the foot of the bed, not touching it, her hands clasped at her back.

Veronika left the room and walked back to the reception. The nurse was back behind the counter. She looked up and presented Veronika with one of her measured, professional smiles. 'It is always difficult, but we manage it well here,' she said. Veronika sat down on one of the chairs in the waiting area. Manage what? she thought. Did either of them have any idea of what was going on inside the room? What was going on between these two people? A dying man and his wife — or a woman with a life to end?

In the end Veronika walked outside and sat on the grass under some birches. It was well over an hour before Astrid came out onto the front steps. She stood there, squinting in the bright light, her hand on the railing, and Veronika walked up to her. She lifted her arms as if to embrace the older woman, but let them fall, allowing one hand only to rest lightly on Astrid's arm as they walked down the stairs. They continued up to one of the benches fronting the dry fountain and the flowerbed and sat down.

'It may take weeks. Or be over today. Nobody knows,' Astrid said. 'The doctor will be here at three.'

They drove to the nearest village for something to eat. There was a choice between a small café and a hotdog outlet. The café was empty and smelled of coffee that had been sitting on the hot-plate for hours. They sat down at one of the small tables with blue and white checked plastic tablecloths. There was no sign of human life. Veronika served them each a mug of scalding bitter coffee from the pot on the counter. As she sat down, a young girl emerged from the interior and they ordered a ham sandwich each. The food arrived quickly and was generous and fresh. Yet Astrid's stayed untouched on the plate while she kept sipping the coffee.

Holding the cup with both hands she looked at Veronika. 'You don't need to stay. I can manage,' she said.

Veronika looked into the old woman's eyes. 'Of course I'll wait. Let's see what the doctor says.'

They drove back to the rest-home and sat in the shade on the bench. Veronika had bought the daily paper, and read it while Astrid sat quietly, her eyes closed. The doctor arrived in a dusty old Volvo station-wagon at a quarter past three. Obviously expecting them, she waved and asked them to follow her inside.

Astrid and Veronika were again taken into the small office. The doctor was young and tanned, dressed in faded jeans and a sleeveless top, as if this was just a short professional interlude in a summer vacation. But she had a kind face and managed to keep any impatience hidden.

'I can't give you the exact time left.' Her accent was not local and Veronika thought that she might be a summer locum. The doctor tried unsuccessfully to make eye contact with Astrid, then turned her eyes to Veronika. 'Your father's heart is weak.' She glanced at the records on the desk in front of her.

She doesn't know the patient, Veronika thought. Perhaps this is the first time she has looked at those records. And this time, she didn't correct the mistaken assumption.

'As I am sure the sister has already told you, it could be a matter of hours. Or days. But not long.' She turned her eyes to Astrid. 'We can arrange for someone from the church to come and sit with you, if you like,' she said. The old woman shook her head but said nothing. 'You may come and go as you like, but during the night we have only one staff member on and it would be best if you either stay for the entire night, or leave at ten o'clock and come back first thing in the morning.'

'I'll stay for the night. I will stay as long as it takes,' Astrid said, with her eyes on the window behind the doctor.

A nurse took them back to the room, then left to get a second chair. They placed both chairs by the window and sat down. Through the closed door they could hear the sounds of soft steps, doors opening and closing, the occasional muted voice. Outside, there were the birds, the odd car passing in the distance. But inside the room it was absolutely silent. Veronika wasn't sure whether Astrid was awake: she was leaning back in her chair with her eyes closed. But at the faintest sound from the bed she would sit up, wide awake and alert. They waited. The light outside dimmed, but the white midsummer night still gave them all the light they required.

The nurse knocked softly on the door before she left at ten. She walked up to the bed and checked the patient, smoothed the immaculate blanket, nodded to the two women and left. A little later the night nurse did the same. She introduced herself, checked the patient and told them to ring if they needed her.

In the silence afterwards, Veronika dozed.

She woke with a start, unable to tell how long she might have slept. Astrid was standing at the foot of the bed, talking quietly. Veronika couldn't hear the words, and remained where she was, still. When she woke the next time, Astrid was by the window. She was a black silhouette against the white dawn outside and she was embracing herself, as if cold. The plastic rustled as Veronika shifted on her seat.

Without turning, Astrid spoke. 'We can leave. It is over.'

Later they drove slowly home along deserted roads. The air was as light as an overcast day, but the absolute stillness could only belong to the night. It was just after one in the morning. They travelled in a world that seemed to have no other inhabitants. It was only when Veronika turned her head to check whether the other woman was awake that she noticed Astrid was crying. Soundlessly, tears ran down her face and fell onto her hands, which sat on her lap, palms up. Veronika averted her eyes and kept them on the road for the rest of the journey.

When she finally stopped outside Astrid's house, the sun was just over the horizon. It was Midsummer's Eve, the longest day of the year. Veronika walked around to the passenger side and opened the door. Astrid sat as before, tears still falling, and Veronika had to take her arm gently and support her as she got out of the car. She held on to the old woman as they walked to the front door.

'Shall I come in for a little while?' she asked as Astrid struggled to find the keys in the pockets of her trousers. There was no reply, but as Astrid walked inside she left the door open. Veronika followed, closing the door behind her.

Astrid stood by the window in the kitchen. The first rays of sunlight darted through the glass, threads of gold weaving through the air and landing on the floorboards.

'They are not for him,' she said. 'My tears. They are not for him. They are for me.'

Veronika walked up to Astrid and took her in her arms. She held her and they stood quietly for a moment.

'Let me help you to bed,' Veronika said.

'Upstairs. I think I will sleep upstairs tonight,' Astrid said. Slowly they navigated the stairs up to the second floor. They crossed the spacious landing, where the morning light played with the dust that their steps stirred, and walked up to the master bedroom. Astrid opened the door and they entered. Still leaning on Veronika's arm, the old woman walked up to the double bed, where the bedspread was folded back from the pillows. She sat down, took off her shoes, then paused for a moment. The white blind covered the window, but the rising light of the new day filtered through, together with the sounds of awakening birds. Astrid pulled up her feet and lay down. She turned towards the wall and curled up foetus-like.

Veronika looked at the old woman's back, the oversized socks, threadbare over her heels. Her narrow back underneath the crumpled shirt. She bent down and pulled off her own shoes then lay down. She adjusted her body to fit behind Astrid's and as the night became day, they lay spooned against each other, wide awake.

'There is a man in Stockholm,' Veronika said quietly. 'His name is Johan. I would like to tell you about him.'

18

Who plays in the night about you and me
On a flute, a little silver flute?
Our love is dead. When did I speak to you.
— A flute, a little silver flute.

Veronika

I have known Johan for such a long time I sometimes forget
that there was a time when I didn't.

He rang me in London to ask me to come home for
Christmas. His voice sounded so close, he could have been
ringing from the next room. I looked at the windows, where
the rain ran like black tears. James's gift to me had been a
new mobile phone, one with a camera. His note had said he
wanted me to see him when he rang. And when he called
from Auckland I had listened to his voice talking about the
sea, about surfing and about blossoms on the lemon tree in

113

his mother's garden, while his smiling face looked back at me from the small screen. Christmas on the beach, barbecues, surfing, sunshine and strawberries. But the words had reached me across a gulf, vague and distant. I had pressed the phone close to my ear, but it was as if the rain falling between us blurred the sound and the images.

I flew from Heathrow three days before Christmas. Johan had offered to meet me at Arlanda airport but I had declined. I wasn't sure if he would be there regardless, and felt relieved when he wasn't. Stockholm was as dark and wet as London, but colder, grey slush covering the streets. I took the bus to the city, then the underground. It was late afternoon and the world was compact darkness, Christmas decorations and streetlights providing surreal relief. The train was packed and smelled sadly of wet wool and perspiration. I got off at Karlaplan and pulled my suitcase behind me through the snow, childishly cherishing every miserable slushy step as icy water seeped into my shoes. I crossed the street and continued up to the glass-panelled front door of the apartment building. I pressed the code on the pad and put my shoulder against the door in a reflex movement to push it open. When I realised it wouldn't give, that the code must have been changed, I felt a jolt of anger — and disappointment.

The chandelier on the other side of the glass spread warm yellow light, but I was outside, my feet wet and numb. Large snowflakes fell sparsely over my head, melting instantly as they landed on my hair and shoulders. I pressed the intercom and Johan answered immediately, as if he had been anticipating the call. I took the lift up to the fourth floor. He stood in the doorway, illuminated from behind, and I could smell cooking. He seemed taller, as if he had grown in my absence. His embrace was light, just a brush of cheek against cheek before he bent down and picked up my suitcase. It surprised me that I noticed he had changed his aftershave.

I followed him inside, registering small additions and changes: a framed print on the wall by the kitchen door, a stool just inside the door, a potted ivy on the kitchen windowsill. The apartment looked the same, yet fundamentally different. I had been away almost a year, but it could have been much longer. I felt as if I had lived there in another life. We had spent a lot of time on the renovation, painstakingly doing everything ourselves, in between studies and work. It was a small apartment — just one large room, kitchen, bathroom and hallway. I had loved the kitchen. There was a large gas stove and we had bought second-hand cupboards — some antique, all free-standing. Nothing was built in.

Now, as I stood in the doorway, watching Johan frying Baltic herring, my favourite dish, I knew this space no longer belonged to me. He had a small pile of cleaned fish on a plate, chopped dill on another, then one with beaten eggs and one with coarse rye flour. He methodically placed two of the small flat fish side by side, cut open and skin-side down, sprinkled some of the dill over them, then salt and pepper, before putting one on top of the other, pressing them together and dipping them in the beaten egg, then turning them in the rye flour. His hands moved deliberately, as if he had rehearsed the process to make sure he would get it right. Next, he pushed the fish onto the spatula and slid them into the hot butter in the pan.

He seemed absorbed in the work, but suddenly he looked up at me, smiling and shrugging his shoulders, as if embarrassed. I smiled back, and walked into the main room. The potatoes boiling on the stove had steamed over the window. He had set the long table for two, the plates straight on the table, no place-mats. A basket with white hyacinths planted in white moss sat on the side by the Christmas candlestick, with all four candles lit. A fire was going in the old tiled stove in the corner. I felt my throat ache as I walked around the room barefoot, my feet slowly warming. Some of Johan's music was playing. I hadn't noticed it from the kitchen, but now I recognised it instantly. He had been very happy when he wrote it, just accepted to the Music Academy. It had been All Saints Day, and we had taken a long walk to Haga and back, past the Northern Cemetery, where thousands of candles flickered in the misty early evening. He had held his arm across my shoulders and told me he had never been so happy. And when we came home he played the tape. The music was like that day: intensely joyous and profoundly serene.

I went to the bathroom and let the tap run while I stood leaning against the hand-basin. Two towels hung on identical hooks: one used, one just unfolded, the creases still sharp. I splashed cold water on my face and rubbed the clean towel against my cheeks.

We sat down to eat, in our usual seats: Johan against the wall, I with my back to the room. I suddenly realised I hadn't seen the cat.

'Where is Loa?' I asked. Johan busied himself serving the fish and took a moment to reply. 'You haven't had her put down, have you?'

He looked up, his grey eyes on my face. 'Of course not.' He put the fish on the table and picked up the bowl of mashed potatoes before saying anything further. 'It's just that we were both so miserable. She would wander around the apartment every single evening, searching, before resigning herself to the fact that you weren't here. And I found myself doing the same. Wandering restlessly, half expecting to find you in bed when I returned. And when I finally managed to put the thought out of my mind for a moment, Loa would reappear, staring at me with a sad, accusing look. If I lay sleepless, I would wake her. If I slept, she would wake me with her restless roaming. We kept reminding each other of our misery constantly.' He poured wine. 'So, I took her to stay with Mother on the island. Two older females, both disillusioned — they seem comfortable together.' He looked up and smiled. 'If you stay, we'll get her back.' Instead of answering, I lifted my glass. He lifted his and stretched out his other hand to touch my arm.

'Anyway, you will all meet at Christmas. Mother has invited us for a traditional vegetarian Christmas dinner. No ham, but lots of fine wine. We'll have to spend the night, of course. It will be cramped, nine of us in her small house. But we'll be together again. Maria and Tobias have come down from Umeå, and Mother has invited her old friend Birgitta and her son Fredrik. And I have asked Simon and Petra. Simon and I have tried to keep the band going, but these last few months we haven't had much time.' He was leaning back against the wall, looking straight at me. 'Unless you have other plans, of course,' he said, and it came across almost apologetic. As if he regretted having let himself get carried away and talk too much.

'No. No, I have no other plans. It sounds lovely. Thank you.' I took a sip of wine, listening to the music.

We finished the meal and cleared the table, doing the dishes as we always used to: Johan washing, me drying. Then he made coffee and we returned to the table. We sat in silence in the flickering candlelight, snow falling outside the dark

window. Johan bent forward and took both my hands across
the table.

'I am so very happy, Veronika. Just at this moment, it is
absolute. It doesn't matter about tomorrow; I am here right
now. With you. And I am happy.'

Later, when I came out of the bathroom he had opened the
window. Snowflakes wafted in and melted into drops of water
on the floor. I pulled back the bed covers and got inside. The
room was dark, illuminated only by streetlight and the dying
flames in the stove. Johan went to the bathroom and I lay still,
my eyes on the snow.

When he returned, he closed the window and the shutters
of the stove. He got into bed like a cat, hardly disturbing the
covers. I had turned onto my side, facing the wall. He lay down
and I caught a faint whiff of toothpaste. I lay still, as did he.
Then I felt his palm on my back. Not insistent. Just slowly
moving down my spine. Then he turned, his back against mine,
the sole of his foot touching mine.

When I woke up, the space beside me was empty, but as
I stretched out my hand I could feel that the sheets were still
warm. I could hear Johan moving about in the kitchen and
I could smell toast. I got out of bed, wrapped myself in the
blanket and crossed to the kitchen. I stood in the doorway
for a moment, watching him. His back was towards me and
he was busy filling a tray with mugs, plates, a basket with
bread, marmalade and cheese. The candles on the table were
lit again. Coffee was dripping through the filter of the electric
percolator. He was wearing his old green bathrobe and the
faded pyjama trousers reached only halfway down his legs.
He was barefoot. I walked up to him and pressed my wrapped

body against his back, arms around his waist. He said nothing, just paused briefly with the bread basket in his hand.

'I'll have to leave soon,' he said as we sat down to eat. I looked towards the window but it gave no indication of the time. It was snowing, but absolutely dark. 'Just wrapping up — it's my last working day before Christmas. We could catch the first ferry tomorrow morning.' I held a mug in both hands, blowing air on the scalding coffee.

'Okay, I'll do a little Christmas shopping, then,' I said. And for the briefest moment I felt a sense of anticipation.

When I stepped out the front door the world was a muted twilight where people walked in ankle-deep snow, lifting their feet like wading birds. The streetlights were still lit, though it was close to ten o'clock.

I walked down Sturegatan, crossed Stureplan and continued along Biblioteksgatan. The shops were opening and there were bright lights in the windows. I crossed Norrmalmstorg, where the Christmas market was hurriedly preparing for the trading climax of the year.

The mobile rang just as I was walking into the NK department store. I struggled to untangle the straps of my backpack and rummage around in the front pocket before the ringing stopped. Flustered I put the phone to my ear. 'Veronika,' I said into the phone, covering my other ear with my hand.

'It's James,' he said. There was a long pause, and I was wondering if the phone had cut off, but then he said, 'I miss you.'

As I stood in the entrance my back was hot from the shop's air heater, while cold air blew on my face. 'James.' I looked out over the street, where cars moved slowly, like giant fish in a fish-tank. The headlights made tunnels in the swirling snow.

'Where are you?' he said.

'I'm in Stockholm. It's Christmas,' I said, hearing how stupid it sounded. 'I decided to come home for the holidays,' I added.

He laughed, and I suddenly remembered the feeling of laughter.

'Come to New Zealand, Veronika. Come here and be with me,' he said. 'It's Christmas here, too. Once a year. And the rest is not bad either. Come and live with me in the new world.' I took the phone from my ear and looked at his face on the screen. His hair had grown, I thought. I lifted my face and let snowflakes land on my skin.

By the time he started to talk again, I had made my decision.

I walked through Kungsträdgården, where rows of elms were outlined in white, as if topped with icing. Skaters filled the small rink, revolving gracefully to recorded music, the air filled with slowly whirling snowflakes. I passed the Opera House and crossed the bridge towards Gamla Stan, the Old Town. The water was steaming and ducks and swans were flocking on the icy crust along the edges, shifting from foot to foot and eyeing passers-by with hungry eyes.

I drifted through the crowds at the market at Stortorget. The air smelled of mulled wine, gingerbread, candles and smoked meat. Huddling together in the centre of the square a small choir was singing Christmas carols a cappella, blowing white mist with every note.

I felt as if my senses had suddenly awakened. As if I were taking note, collecting images for the future. I was leaving. On a whim I had decided to travel to the end of the earth to be with a man I hardly knew. So that I would be able to laugh again.

In the evening we went to Blå Porten. Johan had booked. There were candles on all the tables, and the menu was still the same. His hair was wet and he had a handful of shopping bags with him, which he stuffed underneath his chair. We ordered a bottle of red wine. He sat opposite me, rubbing his hands, and I remembered how his fingers always got so cold. 'My hands are freezing,' he said, with an embarrassed smile, blowing air into his cupped hands. I looked at his face, saving that, too. The grey eyes, the whites whiter than any eyes I had ever known, almost pale blue. The curled fair eyelashes. The long arched nose. The fine blond hair, which might begin to thin soon. It struck me that we must look like a happy couple out for a romantic pre-Christmas dinner. Lovers. Comfortable together.

We ate and talked. In the warm light from the candles it was possible to fend off the outside world for a while. We ordered coffee with whipped cream and the moment loomed, inching closer.

When I told him, I knew that I would never again want to cause someone such grief. Perhaps it was the light playing tricks, but it was like watching someone die. As if suddenly all life went out of his face and body. He sat absolutely still, his eyes wide open. Only his hands moved, clasping and unclasping. Then tears began to fall from his eyes onto his hands. He made no attempt at wiping them away. There was nothing I could say, and we sat in silence while diners at the other tables continued their meals, talking, laughing. As if nothing at all had changed. In the end, he excused himself and went to the restroom. I paid the bill, and stood waiting by the exit with our shopping bags when he came out.

We took a taxi back. When we got home, we sat at the table drinking whisky, not saying much. I suggested that perhaps I shouldn't go with him to his mother's the following day.

He looked at me, saying nothing. After a while he stood up and walked towards the kitchen. 'Let's decide tomorrow,' he said, his back to me.

In the morning, it was as if we had both made the same decision. We knew I wasn't going. Johan went about his packing. 'I'll come with you to the ferry, if that's okay,' I said. He didn't turn to look at me, but asked me to ring for a taxi. It had stopped snowing over night, but the streets were not cleared yet. The whole city was in white padding, all sounds muted. We stood on the quay in front of the Grand Hotel, our feet in the snow, waiting for the ferry gate to open. The sun rose, illuminating some of the old buildings along Skeppsbron across the water. Johan was holding on to the shopping bags with the presents; there was nowhere to put them down. When the gate opened, he turned and put his arms around me, the bags bouncing lightly against the backs of my legs. 'God Jul, Veronika. Merry Christmas, Veronika,' he whispered in my ear. He took a step back, his eyes focused on a spot on the ground between our feet. 'I was wrong, Veronika. I was wrong,' he said, and looked up. 'The moment was never enough. I wanted the future as well.' And he turned and walked on board, never looking back.

19

For sorrow memory was given;
if peace of mind is your demand, forget!

Astrid hadn't stirred and her breathing was light. Except for the buzzing of a couple of drowsy flies on the windowsill, the room was silent. Veronika closed her eyes and continued.

'I left Johan there, and to me he is frozen in time. And all I see is his back. Never his face.'

She paused.

'It is sad to lose the face of a loved one,' Astrid said quietly. 'So sad. We may think it makes it easier, not seeing the face.'

Veronika looked at the back of Astrid's head in front of her. Her hair was swept back from her face, grey strands fanning out on the pillow. Veronika had an urge to stroke her head, but her hands stayed tucked under her chin.

'But it is not true. It makes the pain worse.' Astrid turned onto her back and unconsciously fingered the buttons of her shirt. Then she turned and looked at Veronika.

'I have lost my daughter's face,' Astrid said. 'I could describe every exquisite detail of it. But I can no longer *see* it.' She closed her eyes and as she began to talk her face relaxed, softened, and a hint of a smile set on her lips.

'She had soft coppery hair. Touched by the sun — it shone like my mother's. Her eyes were large and black, but I think they would have become green, just like my mother's. They were so very clear and they looked straight into mine with absolute trust. I would let my finger run over the skin of her forehead and I had never touched anything so soft. When I changed her I put my palm on her chest and stomach, and her eyes locked with mine. I carried her against my body and her hands rested against my chest, connecting with my skin as if she were still a part of me. Her feet kicked against my stomach and the movements were the same as when I carried her in my womb.' Astrid paused. 'There hasn't been a day since she was born that I haven't thought of her. But I can't see her.'

Veronika lay on her back, too, her hands on her stomach.

'Tell me,' she said. 'Let me see your daughter.'

20

With you alone I spoke
what no one else can guess.
On never-ending roads
you were my loneliness.

Astrid

I called her Sara. My mother's name. She was born here in this room. It was February and during the night a snowstorm swept by, piling the snow against the building and closing the roads. I lay awake listening to the howling of the wind and the snow beating against the windows, knowing that my child was about to be born. As the morning broke, the wind died and the sun came out. I stood by the window and looked out and it felt as if the world had just been born. As if the wind and the snow had created a new world for my child.

Eventually, the old midwife made it up the hill through the

deep snow and when my baby was born she was there to help. She put the wrapped little body into my arms and smiled and told me it was a girl. I undid the wrap and ran my palm over the smooth skin of my daughter's body. I held out my finger and her hand grasped it. Her nails were like shiny little fish scales. She held my finger tightly and I looked into her dark eyes. I was filled with such joy that I felt we were invincible, my daughter and I. My daughter Sara.

I put my nose to her neck and took in my daughter's smell. I touched her hair, stroked her cheek, ran my lips over her forehead.

It wasn't until I looked up that I noticed my husband had entered the room. He stood at the foot of the bed, his hands crossed over his chest. The old woman told him he had a beautiful little daughter. He said nothing. His jaws moved, but not a sound came over his lips. His eyes were fixed on the child.

'Red hair,' he said finally. 'She has red hair.' And without another word he left the room.

I carried my child with me everywhere. I felt I knew her every wish, her every need, and she never cried. When the weather grew warmer I carried her with me to the place in the forest. While we walked I told her everything. And I made everything beautiful for her. I told her the beautiful things, for I wanted her world to be good. I wanted to give her a good world. I wanted her to have love and I wanted her to love. We sat in the sun in the enclosed space, and again it was enchanted. Again, the firs stood guard around someone I loved. And for a time the world was truly good.

It rained all May that year, or so it seemed. But rain can be as soothing as sunshine. The mornings were soft, with the fine tapping of spring rain. No, not tapping. It was so light it had no sound. It filled the air and nurtured the new growth soundlessly. I took walks with my baby, carrying her underneath my rain cape. My husband had business in Stockholm and was away most of the spring, but when everything closed down for the summer holidays he came back.

Why can I see all this, when I can't see my baby's face?

I went up the stairs and I knew he was there. The door wasn't closed — all I had to do was push it gently and it swung open soundlessly. He stood leaning over her bed. It is as clear now as it was then. A bright sun shone through the light curtains and it was as if it had come out to make me see every detail.

I walked up to the bed and took her. I held her to my chest, walked down the stairs and then out the front door.

We sat down at the back of the house by the strawberry patch. It was early evening but the sun was still high in the sky. Swallows darted above our heads, hunting for mosquitoes, which had arrived with the warm weather.

We sat on the grass and I held her against my chest with my lips touching the crown of her head. I told her about the strawberries. I promised to thread them onto timothy straws for her. I told her how sweet they would be. How I would pick her a straw for every day of the summer. But as I looked out over the patch, where the flowers were still tight little buds, I knew. I knew that there wouldn't be time.

21

Tonight, you're invited to dance with the mist . . .

The room was darker. The sun had disappeared and gusts of wind rattled the window — a forewarning of rain.

Veronika turned her face and looked at Astrid. She placed her hand gently on the old woman's head, stroking the grey hair, gathering strands behind her ear. She left her hand on the old woman's shoulder and they lay still while the wind rustled the blind.

'It's Midsummer's Eve, but I think it's going to rain,' Veronika said, finally. 'I thought perhaps this afternoon we should walk down to the village and watch the raising of the maypole. I thought it might be a good thing to do. If the rain stops.'

Astrid said nothing, but Veronika could hear her take a deep breath. Veronika sat up and let her feet drop to the floor. She looked at her watch and saw that it was midday, almost noon. She heard Astrid stir behind her, and she stood up to give the old woman room to sit. But she remained lying, turned onto her back.

'Yes,' she said. 'I think that might be just the right thing for us to do.'

She didn't move as Veronika quietly slipped out of the room.

When Veronika returned in the afternoon, she found Astrid sitting on the bench on the porch. She had changed into a white shirt and there was a navy blue woollen cardigan on her lap. Her hair was wet and combed back. Veronika looked at her and thought the old woman was carrying herself differently. There was a subtle change in the angle of her chin, her posture. Resolve, she thought. Dignity. And perhaps relief.

They walked slowly down the hill. The rain had stopped, but it was humid and the sky was overcast. The rain had brought out the smells of the grass and clover. Veronika hooked her arm and invited Astrid to put her arm inside, which she did. As their steps found a common rhythm, the old woman leaned lightly on Veronika's arm.

The open grassy space by the river, beyond the church, was crowded with people, many dressed in the colourful traditional village costume. The women's red skirts swirled and there was a sense of happy anticipation and festivity, even excitement, as the boats approached and faint music could be heard. Four large rowing boats were coming down the river in procession, each with a fiddler accompanying the rowing. Veronika and Astrid stood a little to the side, watching in silence as the boats landed and the crews joined the people gathered on the riverbank and made their way up to where the maypole lay, dressed with birch branches and wild flowers. The fiddlers joined the other musicians who stood ready, and as a team of men started to raise the pole, the fiddlers tuned their instruments. To Veronika it looked like an ancient ritual — heathen, almost. The music was traditional, a little melancholy, yet lively and danceable. And as soon as the pole was upright and secured, adults and children gathered around it, holding hands, and the dancing began.

Astrid stood holding her cardigan with both hands, her eyes on the people moving around the pole in the traditional midsummer songs and dances. She turned to look at Veronika, gave a little nod and a faint smile. She slipped her arm through Veronika's again and they stood together, watching.

After a while Veronika said, 'Let's go and sit over by the river. We can still hear the music and we can see the water.' She had felt the pressure of the old woman's arm on her own grow slowly heavier. As they sat down on the grass, the first rays of the late afternoon sun darted through the opening clouds. Astrid held Veronika's hand while she sat, but seemed comfortable as soon as she had stretched her legs in front of her, down the sloping bank. Veronika gathered her skirt around her legs, already encircled by mosquitoes. She was fanning the air in a feeble attempt at discouraging the insects when Astrid patted her arm.

'Here, have some,' the old woman said, holding out a bottle of roll-on mosquito repellent. 'Midsummer time, never leave home without it,' she said with a little smile. Veronika gratefully applied repellent to her legs, arms and neck.

'We must pick the seven flowers on the way back,' Veronika said. 'Can you remember them from the song?' She looked at Astrid, who looked back with an amused smile.

'Oh, forget-me-not, and timothy grass. And bluebells. Violets?' Astrid paused.

'Yes, and red clover,' Veronika added. 'Cotton-grass. And one more, the one that I can never remember the name of.'

'Yarrow,' said Astrid. 'I read about yarrow many years ago. That the Chinese used the stalks for divination. So I think it is appropriate for your midsummer posy.'

Veronika looked at her with surprise, but Astrid had her eyes on the river, where the late sun now played, sending bright reflections in all directions.

'And who will you dream of, Veronika?' Astrid said, without taking her eyes off the water. 'With the flowers under your pillow. Who?'

Veronika didn't answer. She sat with her legs pulled up and her arms clasped around them, her chin resting on her knees.

'I came here to escape my dreams,' she said eventually.

22

. . . for the day is you,
and the light is you,
the sun is you,
and the spring is you,
and the beautiful, beautiful,
awaiting life is you!

Veronika

But I still dream about the sea. My enemy. I dream about
my enemy, not my love. I dream about the infinite expanse
shimmering in all shades of blue and green, from blackest navy
over unfathomable depths, to bright emerald where the land
below comes closer to the surface.

It lay below me as the plane began its descent over New
Zealand and it seemed to last for ever. If I blinked I could
have missed the tiny sliver of land just risen from the depths.

New Zealand. Aotearoa. But I didn't blink; my eyes were wide open. I felt blank, newly awakened and washed clean, like the windblown land below. I had taken a step off a cliff, not knowing where and how I would land. I pressed my forehead against the window as the plane descended and the land drew closer.

It was early morning and the airport processing was swift. I walked through customs, pushing my luggage trolley, my eyes scanning the wall of faces of the crowd waiting on the other side. But it was he who found me. I felt his hands on my shoulders before I saw him. Then he turned me to face him and held me, and we stood still, an island in the stream of travellers passing by, until an Asian man behind us discreetly asked us to move aside. I looked at James, took in his entire presence: the faded baseball cap over hair that seemed longer and curlier than before, the worn white T-shirt, scruffy shorts, his tanned feet in rubber jandals. His face, where my eyes searched every detail, touching the skin, following the eyebrows, the contours of his lips. Comparing with the stored images. And it all returned to me. Starting as the smallest stirring somewhere deep inside my body, a warmth that spread and reached my limbs, my fingertips, then my lips. My smile felt like laughter.

We walked out into the intense brightness. Thin white clouds stretched across an infinite sky and a fresh wind pushed us along.

We drove towards Auckland. I looked at the passing landscape without registering details. James talked and his left hand pointed out the window, returning to my right knee between each swift movement. I looked at his profile, his hand on the steering wheel, his bare feet on the floor. He looked so perfectly at home, at one with his clothes, his car, the landscape. I realised he was home. And suddenly I became acutely aware of being shrouded in the old world. Out of place, with my winter pale skin, my heavy dark clothes. My body even smelled wrong. Old, tired and out of place in this intensely bright, newly created world where a fresh wind blew and the air had no smell.

We went straight to his mother's house in St Mary's Bay. As we stopped, I looked at the house. A white wooden villa, one of many similar along the quiet street. It looked quaint, like something out of a storybook, but larger than I had imagined. 'My mother lives in a small house in central Auckland,' he had said. I didn't think this looked like a small house, with its large bay windows either side of the front door and a wide veranda running along the entire front and continuing around the corner to the right. White roses spilled over the picket fence and there was a large tree with bright red clusters of round flowers, cheerful, like pompoms bouncing playfully in the wind.

His mother came out the front door as we were unloading my luggage from the boot. She stayed on the top step, her arms down her front, hands clasped. She was small, slim, casually but smartly dressed in white linen trousers and a beige top. Barefoot. Her fair hair was tied back. As I walked up the steps, my eyes searched her face for a likeness to her son. She had large grey eyes, no make-up, a rather long nose, a wide mouth with full lips. I could see no resemblance. She returned my gaze, equally focused, but there was a hint of a smile, potentially even laughter at the corners of her mouth.

'Veronika,' she said, as if deliberately forming the syllables. 'Ve-ro-ni-ka. Welcome to New Zealand. I am Erica.' She embraced me, a soft and swift act, like the touch of a breath of wind. She left her arm on my back, but it was the idea of a soft push rather than the actual physical touch of the arm that guided me through the front door.

We walked through the house and out onto the back porch. The rooms looked like the woman who lived in them — light, airy and attractive. Pleasant, but also private. Not particularly inviting.

James had his room in a sleepout at the bottom of the back garden. He walked ahead of me through the grass, carrying my two suitcases. I looked at his back, let my eyes run along his legs, his arms, his hands. He looked different. Or perhaps just more at home — more genuinely himself. It seemed as if each step he took landed on a spot perfectly fitted for it. I followed, my leather boots trampling the grass insensitively. Inside, I sat down on the low double bed, suddenly tired, even a little sad. He dropped the suitcases, put his hands on his hips and looked at me.

'Tired?'

I nodded.

'Can you manage in the shower, or do you need me to help you?' he said, smiling. 'Hm, I sense that some assistance is required here,' when I didn't answer. Then he threw himself on the bed beside me and started to unbutton my blouse.

We stayed with Erica almost a month. James had found temporary work at the city's underwater aquarium over the summer, with a possible permanent position after that. Although not quite the dream job he was hoping for, it paid the bills. I started to think about my book, writing small patches, while the single cell of the basic idea slowly began to divide and take form and shape.

Erica was away for days at a time, visiting friends at their summer baches and making excursions, so we often had the entire house to ourselves. I spent leisurely hours in the shade on the back porch with Erica's old ginger cat, and in the late afternoon I would walk to the shops to get something for us to eat. Often we ate out, usually at one of the cafés on Ponsonby Road. I had adjusted to the comfort and space, the unhurried, generous atmosphere, and streets with little traffic. It still intrigued me to hear the locals complain about traffic congestion. It seemed to me the embryo of a city, a potential more than a reality. I looked down at the city below, where the Sky Tower stood like a flagpole marking the spot of the centre of a future major city.

After dinner we would come back to the quiet house and sit in the wicker chairs looking out over the garden, while the setting sun painted the city below spectacularly pink, gold and orange, then purple, mauve, until the intensely dark blue of the night took over. We would make love on the old bed in James's room with the folding doors open on to the garden. And it was just as before.

'I was born into the sea; it has surrounded me all my life,' James said. He lay naked on the bed and the cicadas played noisily in the garden. 'To me, the sea is life itself. The colours, the smell. I crave it.' He raised himself onto his elbows. 'Imagine a high wave, a pale emerald green wall, with a school of kahawai chasing smaller fish. The most beautiful picture in the world.' He stretched out his hand and pulled me down on top of him. He held my face in his hands and looked into my eyes. 'I want you to get to know each other. Learn to love each other.'

The next day he took me to Piha to watch him surf. There

are pictures of the New Zealand west coast beaches. They feature in books and films. You can read about the dangers, the unpredictable undercurrents, lethal rips underneath a deceptively calm surface. The force of the surf. But nothing had prepared me properly.

We walked from the car, carrying our mats, the picnic basket and James's surfboard. The vastness was deafening. There were no boundaries, no ends. The beach stretched for ever, dotted only with the odd speck of a visitor. Seagulls hovered in the sky but they never drew close. The scorching light illuminated everything. The sea was everywhere. I walked into the water to my knees, feeling the frightening force of the sea tugging at my ankles, pushing, pulling, ripping. Clawing. James laughed and I could see his mouth move, but the ever-present, never-ceasing thunder of the waves drowned his voice. He pulled at my arms, splashed water at me, laughed and frolicked, while I stood paralysed, feeling the sand being ripped from under my feet.

Afterwards, I sat on my mat, a book on my lap. But my eyes were on James. Even when I took my eyes off the blinding whiteness of the surf and set them on the pages of my book, his image remained. He was out there, a small black shape on a white board, and the image was ingrained on the inside of my eyelids. Dipping between the waves, disappearing for minutes that felt like small eternities. The cluster of swimmers kept between the flags, but the surfers drifted off to the right. When finally he returned, dripping with water and laughter, I felt my hands finally release their grip on the book, stiff and sore.

January was hot and sunny and we spent most weekends on the beach. But it never got any easier. The sea became my enemy. We were fighting over the same man.

In February we moved into a rented house just a few streets

away. Erica never questioned the decision and gave no hint of whether she was disappointed or pleased. Still, it was with a sense of guilt that I realised how relieved I felt once we were in our own home. It was a typical old Ponsonby cottage: a lounge, a bedroom and a study. A small neglected back garden with a lemon tree. The back porch gave a glimpse of the sea if we stood and craned our necks.

On our first evening in the house we sat on the floor of the porch, smoking and drinking beer. We had worked hard all day and it had been hot. I felt deliciously tired — physically exhausted, yet mentally alert. And so very happy.

'We could live here all our lives,' James said. 'With our kids, cats and dogs.'

'Kids?' I said, and it surprised me how absolutely comfortable I felt with the thought of children. Our children.

'Our children,' he said, bending over to kiss my stomach before pressing his ear against the skin. 'Here — this is where we will plant them,' he said. 'Our children.'

I closed my eyes and rested my head against the wall, running my fingers through his hair.

'I want everything to be just like this, always,' he said moving his hands to my legs, running his palm along my thighs, shins. 'I love you,' he said and my body listened with every cell.

And as the sun sank below the hill behind us the city lost its colours to the falling night. The sound of innumerable invisible cicadas closed in and the air was streaked with the fragrance of equally invisible flowers, and we became one, with each other and with the surrounding night. Afterwards, as we lay on the floor, my eyes looked up into the soft darkness above, where unfamiliar stars flickered. My head rested on his shoulder with my nose tucked into the space just below his ear. I breathed the smell of his body and I stroked the skin of my stomach with my hand. And I thought of the children I knew we would have.

23

. . . but all in my life, like sunshine bright,
and all that sank into pain and night
trembles tonight on a flood of light.

The sky had cleared completely and the grassy area where the midsummer celebration was now at its peak lay washed in the bronze of the evening sun. Clouds of mosquitoes followed the dancers around the maypole, conducting their own intricate airborne dance over the heads of the people. The music from the violins and the accordion blended with the sound of invisible crickets, the occasional cry of a small child. There was laughter from shadowy groups of young people which seemed to mushroom at the fringes of the open area, near the obscurity of the dark trees beyond.

'Shall we walk back?' Veronika said. Astrid nodded and accepted both Veronika's hands to help her stand. They walked arm in arm along the river for a while, then left the bank and continued on the unsealed road towards the church. The odd car and moped passed by.

'I have some herring and gravlax,' Astrid said. 'Would you like to share a light supper with me when we get back?' Veronika tightened her hold on Astrid's arm a little as she answered.

'I would love to.'

They carried on, a solitary couple walking against the flow, away from the festivities. The potato fields lay lush and green on either side of the road, the plants earthed up and the white flowers opening. As they approached the church, Astrid slowed her steps. 'There is something I need to do here,' she said, indicating the church. They walked up the gravel path and Astrid led the way along the side of the building into the churchyard behind. She walked up to the largest headstone. It lay in semi-darkness, now that the low setting sun was obscured by the church building.

The tall, dark headstone sat in the centre of a grassy square, fenced with a heavy iron chain attached to poles at the four corners. A miniature willow with dark purple foliage leaned towards the headstone on one side. There were no flowers. The headstone itself was polished black granite and the inscription stated that it was the Mattson Family Grave.

'Karl and Britta were my grandparents,' Astrid said, her eyes on the first set of names on the stone. 'As you can see, they died within a year of each other. My grandfather bought the grave for perpetuity — the same as his intention when he built the house. A house for life, a house for death. Both the grandest in the village. My father, Karl-Johan, is the only other person buried here.' Astrid shifted her stance and leaned a little more heavily on Veronika's arm.

'My mother was buried in Stockholm. I have never seen her grave.' She was silent and the noise from the distant midsummer festivities floated on the air. 'Now I will bury the last person in this grave. My husband. And then it will be sealed for ever.'

Astrid turned and pulled Veronika with her. They walked slowly over to the other side of the churchyard, near the stone wall. There were no headstones here, just small plaques embedded in the grass. Astrid stopped and knelt awkwardly, holding on to Veronika's hand. She wiped the plaque in front of her with the palm of her hand.

'This is where I buried my daughter Sara,' she said. 'And this is where I will rest.' She indicated the empty space to the left. 'This is our house.'

The two women sat in silence. Veronika brushed away the odd mosquito from her face. Finally, Astrid moved to stand. 'I thought you should know,' she said. 'I wanted you to see where my daughter is.' She took Veronika's arm again. 'And I wanted you to know where I will be.'

They walked back out onto the road. The light was warm, like the air. They could still hear the music in the distance. 'The flowers. You must pick your midsummer flowers,' Astrid said as they turned onto the road up the hill. 'Let's see if we can find them all.'

They took their time, leaving the road and walking in knee-high grass where the dew was beginning to set. They found bluebells, violets, red clover, timothy grass, lily of the valley, meadow saxifrage.

'I have six — only one more,' Veronika said. 'And I really should have a yarrow.' She bent down over a patch of the insignificant white flowers, with their light medicinal smell, and picked one. 'That's it. I have seven now,' she said. As they again stepped onto the unsealed road they each had a small posy of seven flowers. They wandered slowly home, Astrid panting a little.

As they stopped by Astrid's gate, Veronika put her arm on the old woman's. 'Let me get some wine,' she said. 'I'll put these under my pillow, too. Just so I don't forget later tonight.' Astrid nodded and opened the gate.

When Veronika returned a little later, she had two bottles of wine, one under her arm and one in her hand, and a small portable CD player in the other. Astrid was washing new potatoes in the kitchen sink. On the table, her small posy sat in a glass. 'Mine doesn't belong under my pillow,' Astrid said. 'No more dreams for me.'

Veronika put the bottles on the table and then connected the CD player. 'I thought you could keep this,' she said. 'I usually play my music on my laptop.' Astrid turned and looked at her, a potato in one hand and the small brush in the other. 'I wasn't sure what music you like, so I brought a few. This here is Brahms.'

As the music from the small box filled the room, Astrid stepped away from the sink and slowly sat down on one of the kitchen chairs, potato and brush still in her hands and water dripping onto her lap. 'What is it?' she asked quietly. 'This music, what is it?'

Veronika looked at the old woman, taken aback by her reaction. 'It's the sonata for violin and piano, No. 3 in D minor,' she said. As the first notes of the second movement sounded, Astrid put the potato and brush on the table in front of her and folded her hands in her lap.

'My mother used to play it so often I knew every bar. But it's been so long. Such a long time of silence.' She closed her eyes and seemed to listen intently.

When the last movement finished, Astrid looked up. 'And there is the hoya,' she said, her eyes on the potted plant on the windowsill. The long stems framed all of one side of the window, carrying clusters of pink flowers. 'The first flowers just opened the other day. Have you seen the buds? So hard, polished like pearls. You would never think they could contain such velvety softness. Such sweet perfume.' She looked at Veronika. 'Sorry,' she said. 'It's the music. It's been over seventy years since I heard it. Yet it comes back to me now and I realise it was always there. In my heart. All these years I have had it, here, inside, without knowing.' She put her palm on her chest, leaving a wet spot on her shirt. 'My mother used to play it on her gramophone. And the second movement was her favourite. She would play it again and again, telling me to listen carefully, because she said the music contained all the beauty in the whole world. She would sit me on her lap and I would put my ear to her chest and it was as if the music came from inside Mother's body.' Astrid stretched out her hand for the potato. 'Can you please play it again?' she said as she stood and returned to the sink.

And with the Brahms sonata filling the kitchen, they went about preparing their midsummer dinner.

Later, they sat by the table with the window open to the summer night. Astrid had lit a mosquito coil on the windowsill and a thin trail of smoke drifted towards the ceiling. The smoky smell blended with the sweet honey perfume of the hoya.

'Can you please play the second movement again, Veronika,' Astrid said. 'Just once more.' She stretched out her hand and let her fingers touch the midsummer posy in the small vase on the table. She kept her eyes on the flowers as the music swelled again.

Veronika sat leaning against the back of her chair, eyes closed, turning her wine glass in her hand. Both women remained still after the music finished. Then Astrid withdrew her hand from the flowers and looked up.

'I killed the music,' she said. 'And I killed my child.'

24

. . . for nothing hurts like you.

Astrid

I died that summer night.

I sat in the grass at the back of the house with my baby in my arms. The white clover smelled of honey: it was the time in the afternoon when it is easy to drowse and slip into light summery dreams. I fed my baby until she fell asleep on my breast. Her lips let go of the nipple and her head tipped backwards a little on my arm. Her mouth was slightly open with a thin trail of milk at the corner. I wiped it away with my finger. I ran my little finger over her soft gums and felt the tips of the two new teeth, like embedded grains of rice. Her eyelids were closed, the finest film over her black eyes. They fluttered now and then and her lips quivered in fleeting secret smiles.

When I heard his steps on the front porch I stood and

walked away downhill over the meadow. I held her in my arms and talked to her. I pointed out the flowers, the bees, the swallows high above. I held her close to my chest and I could feel her lips against my skin.

I headed towards the river, but then changed my mind and walked uphill again. The high grass rustled against my legs. I whispered to her that the bluebells were just opening. I walked with her in my arms over the meadows and into the forest. The light was gentle and the air still underneath the branches, and it smelled of resin. The soft moss silenced my steps. We passed the large granite block but I didn't stop. I had nothing to pray for this time. When I reached the clearing I sat down on the silken grass where the wild strawberries had just opened their white flowers. I rocked her gently while I sang her all my lullabies. I made her comfortable on my lap, with her head resting on my thighs and her feet against my stomach. Her hands held my fingers in a tight grip and I looked into her black eyes. I bent forward, put my lips to her forehead and blew softly, then let them brush over the crown of her head, touching her heartbeats through the downy membrane.

When the sun dipped behind the wall of trees we lay down on the grass. The air was beginning to cool and I could hear the sounds of the approaching night. The hushed rustling of leaves as invisible animals began to stir. My baby slept in my arms, her breath so soft I had to put my ear to her mouth to feel it.

Then I put my hand over her face and the white night swallowed us.

Afterwards, I sat with her body in my arms, rocking. I screamed into the night until my voice broke. Then all was still.

With the first morning sun I walked back to the house with

her body in my arms. I went upstairs into the bathroom and undressed her. Her body was light on my arm and her skin so white. I washed her with water from my cupped hand. Droplets fell into the pool of water in the hand-basin, like tears. When I had finished I wrapped her in a soft bath towel, walked into the bedroom and took out her baptism gown. I dressed her and brushed her wet hair. I held her close and touched her hair with my hand. When I put my lips on her head all I could smell was the faint perfume of the soap.

I put her in her bed and smoothed the blanket. Then I went downstairs and into the kitchen where my husband sat at the table.

'Your child is dead,' I said.

And afterwards there was only silence.

25

Grief, its shadow in the room
doesn't move with the sun
doesn't become dusk
as dusk begins to fall.

Astrid's face was ashen. Though her eyes were dry, they reflected such grief that Veronika had to avert her own eyes. She rose, walked around the table and gently pulled Astrid to her feet. She embraced the old woman, held her tightly in her arms while she whispered softly in her ear.

'Oh, Astrid,' she breathed. 'My dearest, dearest Astrid.' She let her hand stroke the old woman's hair, then pulled back a little and looked into her eyes. With a sudden inhalation, Astrid turned around to face the window, and with her hands over her mouth she tried to stifle the sound that came from her lips. A cry of such enormous pain it seemed unbearable.

Unbearable to release, and unbearable to hear. Unconsciously, Veronika's hands rose and covered her ears for a moment, before they moved to her mouth in an attempt to silence the sounds of her own crying. Then she moved forward until her body was just behind Astrid's and she embraced the old woman from behind. They stood by the window, closely together, while the sun rose and threw its first rays across the table, where the midsummer flowers sat in the small vase.

Astrid's uncontrollable sobs slowly turned into a gentle rocking of both their bodies. Eventually, Astrid stretched out a hand, groping for the back of her chair. Veronika let go of her shoulders and they both sat down.

'Since that night, I have never once allowed myself to cry for my daughter,' Astrid whispered. 'Not when she was buried. Not on her first birthday. Never.' She put her hands over her mouth, as if trying to stop the flow of words. When she let them sink back onto the table she opened her mouth again. 'And I never cried for myself, either. For the little girl who was me. Or for the young woman I grew up to become.' Astrid paused. 'If there is no comfort to be had, tears have no purpose.'

She stood, walked over to the stove, took the tea-towel and wiped her eyes. She stood by the stove, her eyes on the window, her hands twisting the tea-towel.

'I have never allowed myself to even touch on this before. I buried all thoughts together with my daughter. It hurts so . . .' She pressed the towel to her mouth. 'You see, it was me. It was always about me. Because my love wasn't strong enough.' She crossed the floor slowly and sat down again. 'I couldn't be sure. I couldn't be sure I would be strong enough. And if I couldn't be sure, then it could all have happened again. I think that is how it was. But perhaps that is not the truth. Perhaps it wasn't that my love wasn't strong enough. Perhaps it was that my hatred was too strong.'

She stared straight ahead, her profile a silhouette against the light outside the window. 'And that is an unbearable thought,' she said quietly. She turned to Veronika. 'I am sorry you had to see this. Hear this.'

Veronika stretched out her hand and let it touch the old woman's cheek. 'Let me help you to bed,' she said.

They walked slowly up the stairs, Astrid leaning on Veronika's arm and with her other hand on the banister. Astrid lay down fully clad and Veronika pulled a blanket over her. She brushed her cheek again and crossed the floor to the window, where she pulled down the blind. When she turned back Astrid's eyes were closed. Her face was very pale. Veronika sat down in the chair near the window. The room was in morning twilight and the only sound was the odd sudden soft, stifled sob, like that of a small child that has cried itself to sleep.

But Astrid was not asleep. She had turned onto her side and she lay with her hands tucked under her pillow and her eyes on Veronika.

'I have never talked to anyone about that night. Ever,' she said. 'And now when I listen to my own words, I realise that they tell a different story from the one I have carried all these years.' The old woman closed her eyes. 'I think that if we can find the words, and if we can find someone to tell them to, then perhaps we can see things differently. But I had no words, and I had nobody.'

'Yes,' Veronika said. 'Perhaps I should try to find the words, too. I am a writer, yet words have never come easily to me. Only with great difficulty. And only written ones. I came here with my manuscript unwritten. Now I think that there will perhaps be a book, but not the one I thought I would write.' She looked across at Astrid, but she could not tell whether she was awake. Her white face expressed no emotion and the eyes were closed. Still, Veronika continued to talk.

'You see, I went to New Zealand thinking I would pick up more or less where my last book finished. Thinking I would write a book about place, about home. About love, and how love can give a sense of belonging. But it was never that easy. First, I had to give myself — give us — time to settle. I had to develop my own way of looking at his world. And I thought I had all the time in the world.'

She stopped talking and stared into the space between herself and the old woman.

When Astrid opened her eyes and looked straight at her, she continued.

'Let me tell you when my time ended.'

26

I whisper 'Yes' and 'Always', as I lie
Waiting for thunder from a stony sky.

Veronika

It was the first weekend of November and the summer that had
never quite ended began again. The days were warm, but the
nights still cool. It was early morning and it was Saturday.

While I lay quietly waiting for James to wake up, I pressed
my leg against his, absorbing his warmth through my skin.
He lay on his stomach, arms outstretched, one over the edge
of the bed, the other across my chest. His breathing was soft,
almost inaudible. I heard the morning paper being tucked
into our mailbox just outside the window, which was pulled
up an inch or two. I could see that it was light, but I had
not yet learned to interpret the shades of daylight. Southern
Hemisphere November light. Late spring or early summer, so

unlike any November I had known before. Here, it was as if summer and winter were intertwined: there was summer in the midst of winter, winter in the midst of summer. And there was no autumn, no spring, no time for anticipation, no time for remembrance. Only the present. Or perhaps I had just not yet developed the sensitivity required to distinguish the subtle season changes. I still had three unexplored months before my first year in New Zealand would be complete.

There was an almost imperceptible change in the rhythm of James's breathing and I knew he was awake. His hand on my chest moved and cupped my breast. I turned and faced him as his eyes opened.

His eyes were always wide open when we made love, looking straight into mine. Like those of a small child, they expressed every shift of emotion: passion, pleasure, excitement, tenderness. And joy, always joy.

We stayed in bed until hunger drove us out. In the kitchen we opened the doors to the veranda and took our coffee and toast outside. The sky was clear, with only the occasional light cloud dissolving in the high wind. It was still cool, but you could sense that the day would be warm.

'Ah, what a day. Let's go to the beach,' James said, standing on the steps leading down into the garden, his eyes on the sky.

Then, the words that would change everything. My words.

'All right.'

Just the two. There are so many others I could have chosen. I could have said, 'No, let's take the ferry to Waiheke and go bicycling.' Or 'Let's walk down to Cox's Bay.' Or 'Let's walk into town, go to the art gallery, have lunch.' Or just 'No,

I don't really feel like the beach.' I could have said, 'I think I am pregnant.'

Instead, all I said was, 'All right.'

While I showered, James started to prepare lunch. Bread, eggs, olives, tomatoes. Mussels, cheese. Beer and water. I stood in the doorway watching him putting everything together. I watched his hands and felt an urge to hold them, to put them on my body. He grinned and stuck an olive in his mouth.

On the way, we stopped at a petrol station to fill the car and get some ice for the chilly-bin. Traffic was light as we drove west. We had decided on Karekare and as we turned off the main road onto the meandering steep drive down to the beach I was again struck by the view. Lush green bush, reminiscent of a tropical forest yet distinctly different. It looked new. Raw, recently created, but at the same time prehistoric and untainted by humans. I felt as if I could still see the structure, the overall shape of the land, before it was inhabited.

At the bottom of the road there were small houses with defiant flowerbeds of petunias and geraniums. There seemed to be no connection between these quaint dwellings and the stark landscape. Even on such a cheerful, bright, early summer day Karekare was haunting, awe-inspiring, and to me the small houses seemed out of place, as if they had been conceived with an entirely different, safe, ordinary environment in mind. This seemed a place to admire more than love, I thought. It inspired a spiritual reaction, an acute awareness of human insignificance.

We parked and unpacked and, with our arms full, waded across the stream and onto the black sand, already warm under our feet. The beach was almost empty, with a group of lifesavers assembled around a four-wheel-drive bike and an inflatable rescue boat. The flags were up.

The sea crashed onto the sand and a fine gauze of sea spray softened the view over the shimmering expanse beyond. We spread our mats and James opened the beach umbrella and secured it in the sand. We sat for a while, looking out over the sea. Seagulls screamed high overhead. And this is the next point where my words might have changed everything.

'Feel like a little swim?' he said.

I could have said, 'Okay, for once I think I will.' Or 'Yes, but I'll only go in to my knees.' Or I could have said, 'James, I think I am pregnant.' Instead, I said, 'You know I don't really like swimming here. You go; I'll stay here and read.'

He pulled on his wetsuit and again sat for a moment beside me. I was on my stomach, my book open in front of me. I was rereading *The Werewolf* by Axel Sandemose. I had been thinking of interweaving the story with the narrative of my own book. I was reading carefully, focusing on structure, a pencil in my hand.

'It's perfect,' James said, squinting as he looked out over the sea. I half turned, leaning on my elbow to follow his gaze, but then lay down again. 'We'll eat when I'm back,' he said, and I felt him bending over and pressing his lips onto a spot at the nape of my neck. I smiled to myself, but I didn't turn. I didn't see him pick up the board and wander across the sand down to the water. I didn't see him wade into the water, drift seawards, catch the first wave.

You told me, Astrid, that it is impossible to say what it is that makes you *know* that summer has peaked. That one day, when the sun is as high in the sky as the day before, the water as warm, the grass as green, you just *know*.

I lay on my blanket and read, then rested my head on my arms and dozed off. But as abruptly as if I'd been doused in icy water, I woke. I *knew*. It wasn't the stretch of time that had passed. Nor were there any alarms, any screams. The sky was still blue, the seagulls still circled high above. A woman played with a dog on the flat mirror of wet sand along the edge of the water. But I *knew*.

I stood and with my hands shielding my eyes I looked out over the sea. There was a small cluster of swimmers well inside the flags, and a few a little further off. A couple of young boys were chasing a frisbee. But there were no surfers.

In silence my body began to move. My feet landed on the black sand as they picked up speed, running towards the lifeguards. I was racing, but the world around me moved in slow motion, holding me back. The first lifeguard turning to face me, then screaming to the others, their swift movements getting the rescue boat into the water and jumping on board. To me, it all took place in absolute silence and with unbearable slowness.

I ran down to the water, my eyes on the orange boat zigzagging through the breaking waves. People gathered around me but they were in another world, on the other side of a gigantic gulf that swallowed all sound. Water splashed around my feet as I ran along the beach, following the direction of the boat. A girl in a yellow lifeguard T-shirt ran beside me, her arm reaching out to catch mine. The boat was now further from shore and dipping out of view between the waves. I felt my teeth begin to chatter as I stopped and stood in ankle-deep water. The girl in the yellow T-shirt put her arm around my shoulders and we stood silently, our eyes on the thundering sea, where the boat was now an orange speck.

I felt as if all stood still, as if my own breathing had stopped. Then I saw the boat returning, still dipping in and out of view, but each time emerging a little closer. And suddenly I could sense the lack of urgency. It was no longer a rescue operation.

They carried him up to the makeshift lifeguard base and placed him on a blanket. There were no attempts at CPR or mouth to mouth. The lifeguards stood back and I fell to my knees, my hands reaching out to touch him. I licked the salt water from his eyelids. I put my ear to his chest. I whispered into his ear, the words of our entire life. I put my ear close to his mouth and listened for an answer. Above us the pitiless sun, while the world swirled incomprehensible around the stillness that was the two of us. Then the violent crashing of the victorious sea.

There was a small cut above his left eyebrow and a deep scratch along the length of his left arm. That was all. His head had fallen to the side facing me. I put my hands on his cheeks, bending down to press my own against his. I lay down beside him, stroking his hair.

Eventually, someone gently pulled me up and the girl in the yellow T-shirt wrapped a blanket around my shoulders. There were people gathered around us, their faces pale moons, some crying. They put him on a stretcher and carried him up to the clubhouse. I walked slowly and it surprised me that others were running. There was loud talk, screaming. I noted the commotion with detached surprise.

I sat on a chair in the bare lifeguard clubhouse, a cup of scalding tea on the table in front of me. Around me, there was a world to which I no longer belonged. It was if a heavy door had shut with a sigh and left me outside, alone. I could remember the morning, making love, packing, driving to the beach, but it seemed as if in another time. When I was still alive.

27

But then I want to be alone,
rocked by the flood of light
onto the peaceful rest,
where there is neither wrong nor right.

Astrid lay still, tears streaming down her face to her pillow. She made no attempt at wiping her face; her hands remained tucked underneath the pillow. Veronika stood and pulled up the blind. Outside, the sun was gently awakening the wind. The light reflected on her face and she closed her eyes.

'The shortest night of the year. Midsummer's night,' she said. 'And here is the new day.'

She turned and walked up to the bed, bent over and placed a quick kiss on Astrid's forehead. The old woman pulled out her hand and stroked Veronika's cheek, but she said nothing. Veronika walked across the room and as she opened the door she threw a quick glance over her shoulder, but Astrid had pulled up the blanket and turned towards the wall. Veronika closed the door softly behind her.

On the Monday after midsummer weekend Veronika took Astrid to the rest-home where they had arranged to meet the undertaker. He had initially suggested meeting at his office in town, a good hour's drive away. Alternatively, he had offered to come to Astrid's house. But Astrid had insisted on meeting at the rest-home. Neutral ground, perhaps.

When Veronika drove up to Astrid's gate, Astrid was waiting on the porch. She came down the path wearing her usual outfit: trousers and a large shirt. Yet somehow she looked serene. Her hair was brushed back from her face and her eyes were sharp and very blue as they set on Veronika's face. 'Thank you,' she said, before getting into the passenger seat.

They had plenty of time and Veronika had chosen the slightly longer route, the old road that meandered through the small villages, rather than the highway. Wild flowers covered the road verge and the groves of birches rustled their fresh green heads in the air. Every little village had its own maypole, still standing in a central spot.

They drove up outside the home with ten minutes to spare, but the undertaker stood waiting on the front steps. He was middle-aged, completely bald, but with thick bushy eyebrows and a beard to compensate. He wore a short-sleeved, open-neck white shirt and light slacks — an informal yet somehow appropriate outfit. His handshake was firm and professional.

They sat down in the visitors' area by reception. The nurse offered coffee, but they all declined. Once Astrid had confirmed that she wanted a church ceremony, the date was set to Friday. When the undertaker started to ask for specific instructions, Astrid raised her hand. 'I will leave that to you,' she said. 'I have no interest in the ceremony at all. As long as it takes place in the village church. No cremation. A burial, simply. In the Mattson family grave.' The undertaker took notes but made no comment. It was over in fifteen minutes.

As they were about to leave, the nurse approached, a plastic carry-bag in her hand. 'Mr Mattson's belongings,' she said, and held out the bag. Astrid took a small step back, her hands on her chest, and shook her head. 'Do what you like with it,' she said. 'I don't want it.' The nurse stiffened visibly, but said nothing. She nodded, forced a little smile and took refuge behind the reception desk. Veronika looked at the small bag, which the nurse had dropped on the floor beside her chair. It lay flat, clearly not containing much.

They drove back slowly, the main road this time, with the car windows open. It was midday and the sun sat high in the sky. The road lay empty before them, shimmering in the heat.

'Let's go swimming in the lake when we get back,' Veronika said with a quick look at Astrid. The old woman returned her gaze, eyebrows raised in surprise.

'Swimming?' she said, and turned her head away, looking out over the passing landscape. Her hair blew around her head and she had her arm resting on the window frame.

'Yes,' she said after a while, without turning her head. 'Let's do that. Let's go to the lake.'

They stopped at their houses to collect towels and Veronika made a couple of sandwiches while Astrid filled her blue thermos with coffee.

There were no other cars parked at the end of the narrow road down by the lake, just two bicycles, one a child's. When they walked onto the sand reef it looked completely deserted, but then they saw a woman and a little boy down by the water on the far side. They spread their blanket and sat down, out of sight of the other two swimmers. They could see no sign of human life anywhere and there were no buildings visible along the shores. The lake was still and the dark forest across the expanse was reflected on the surface. The water lapped softly onto the red sand. Veronika took off her shorts and T-shirt to expose a green one-piece swimsuit. Astrid sat fully dressed, in trousers and a white shirt, but barefoot, her legs stretched out in front of her. From her bag she produced a faded cotton sunhat, which she pulled over her hair. That done, she sat with her hands resting on her lap, gazing out over the still water.

'Are you coming in?' Veronika asked as she stood up. Astrid just shook her head, her eyes fixed on a point in the distance across the lake. Veronika waded into the water, treading cautiously over a stretch of pebbles before reaching soft sand a little further out. In knee-deep water she turned and waved to Astrid, who made no gesture in return. The warm water was golden brown, coloured by the mineral-rich soil. She could see her feet through the water, distorted and yellowy. She walked on through the slowly rising water. When it reached her waist, she began to swim. She turned and floated on her back, carried by water that felt silken against her skin. Above, the sky domed, infinite and bright blue. She turned and dived, and when she emerged the water on her lips tasted of metal.

When she walked up to the blanket where Astrid sat immobile she shook her hair and water sprayed lightly over the old woman. 'You should go in — it's wonderful!'

Astrid said nothing, looking out over the water. But when Veronika sat down, the old woman looked at her, a hint of a smile in her eyes. 'I have no swimsuit,' she said. 'And I can't swim.'

Veronika lay down on the blanket and closed her eyes to the sun. 'It's my birthday next week. Perhaps we should make a trip to the city and do some shopping. We could get you a swimsuit. And then we could have lunch at a little place I have heard about on the way back. Celebrate a little.' She pulled herself up onto her elbows. 'Would you come with me and help me celebrate my birthday?'

Astrid busied herself pouring coffee into two plastic mugs. She said nothing. Only when she had closed the thermos and handed Veronika her mug, did she look up.

'I would like that very much. After the funeral,' she said. 'We'll go after the funeral. And I will buy a swimsuit.' She lifted her cup, stuck a piece of sugar in her mouth and smiled, her lips tightly closed. 'And then we will celebrate.'

'The funeral,' Veronika said slowly. She sat up and looked at Astrid. 'Are you frightened?' she asked. The old woman sat as before, her legs stretched out in front of her and her eyes on the distant surface of the lake. She shook her head slowly.

'No,' she said. 'I am not frightened. And I am not sad. Not any more. It is all over. The ceremony will just be the final gesture. Closure.' Astrid had set her mug on the sand. 'I know now that it was myself I was afraid to face. As I stood by my husband's bed and watched his last breaths, it was as simple as blowing out a candle.' She paused, her eyes on the lake. 'There was nothing more to be afraid of.' Then she turned and looked at Veronika. 'Because it was never about him. It was about me.'

Veronika lay with her eyes closed, her fingers digging into the sand.

'Someone told me that there is comfort in a funeral,' she said. 'That the ritual provides an opportunity for the grieving to come to terms with the loss. That is not how it was for me.' She sat up and stretched out her legs beside the old woman's, her eyes vacant, although set on the same blue hills beyond the lake.

'For me, there was no comfort to be had.'

28

Oh, how can I quiet my heart,
That is tossed from north to south?

Veronika
She walked slowly, like someone walking a tightrope over a fathomless gulf. I stood as she approached down the long hospital corridor, and the linoleum was cool and soft against my soles. I was still barefoot, dressed in my swimsuit and with a blanket over my shoulders. My legs were covered in a fine dust of dried salt. I was cold — so cold it felt as if I would never be warm again. As she came closer I could sense that she didn't see me. Her face was very pale and her eyes empty. A woman I vaguely recognised followed. She didn't touch Erica, but stayed close behind. A nurse came out to receive them and Erica's eyes met mine for a second, but there was no sign of recognition and she said nothing. I began to lift my

hands, but let them fall again as she turned to the nurse, who took her elbow and led her into the room. I sat down on the bench again.

In the afternoon, when I came back to the house, I pulled on his red bathrobe and lay down on the bed. I turned and buried my face in his pillow, where his smell still lingered.

He was buried on the Wednesday. Erica's friend came around the Monday before. I heard the knocking, but it took me several minutes to understand the implication. The sound seemed as meaningless as everything else that might be happening in the world beyond the twilight where I lay. Irrelevant and requiring no response. Eventually, she used the key that Erica had given her. Her name was Carolyn. She made tea and sat on the bed and talked to me. She told me about the arrangements that Erica was making and asked me if I had any objections. I looked at her kind face, but I was unable to make any connection with her words. I pulled the bathrobe close, still unable to get warm.

When I think about it now, I wish there had been more time. I feel that grief has its own organic processing time, which cannot be compressed without consequences. Given time to take its course, perhaps the healing is more complete. As it was, the twilight never lifted. Inside my house, time had another dimension and there was neither day nor night, just a continuous stretch of twilight.

On the day of the funeral I walked up the aisle behind Erica and James's father, who had flown in from London, but I was somewhere else, somewhere where the light didn't reach. They were holding hands, a couple united in their grief. I saw them, I registered everything, yet it seemed to have nothing to do with me.

There were friends from school, friends from university, from work. There were relatives. They all seemed to belong, seemed to have a place in the fabric that had been James's life. I walked along the pews filled with people who were almost all unknown to me. There was a man about James's age whose face turned to me as I passed. He was crying and wiping his tears with the back of his hand. I had never seen him before and had no idea of his relationship with James. And he would never know the James that had been mine. Yet we were both grieving for the loss of the same man. I felt my steps get softer and softer, as if I were no longer touching the floor. And I was still so very cold.

I had declined to read, but in my head the words of the poem I had considered kept repeating themselves:

> All, all that I had
> Was yours more than mine.
> All my best intentions
> Were thine, thine, thine.

I had attempted to translate Karin Boye's poem, but, struggling with the words, I had suddenly realised that they were for James, and for me, and that a translation was superfluous. They had nothing to do with this funeral, with these people. I could read them to him in my mind and the language didn't matter.

Afterwards, there was a gathering at Erica's house. I wandered through the rooms, filled with people I had never met before, and sat down on the steps of the back porch. The old ginger cat was asleep in its usual spot. There were people all around, but the cat slept undisturbed, and I sat in solitary

171

silence. Then I heard steps behind me and when I looked up I saw James's father approaching. He sat down beside me. We had been introduced at the church, but I had registered nothing about him. Now I looked into his face and I could see the whisper of a resemblance. I wondered if what I saw was a likeness of how James would have come to look. He put his hand over mine and his eyes searched my face.

'I am sad we will not get to know each other,' he said. He sighed and his hand stayed on mine for a moment. I could think of nothing to say. Eventually, he rose awkwardly and I realised he was older than the overall impression implied. A handsome, well-kept man, considerably older than Erica. I remembered James telling me that his mother had become pregnant while in London on a scholarship to the Royal Ballet. That his father had been married, and that there had never been a question of his leaving his family. I looked at the old man now and wondered whether his regrets were about never getting to know his son, rather than me.

I walked back to our house in the early evening. It was still light and warm. I passed the tennis courts and I could hear the sounds of games, balls bouncing against racquets, players shouting, laughter. Along Ponsonby Road the doors of the restaurants were open to the approaching evening and people were sipping wine at the tables on the pavement. Wherever I looked, there was life. But in my still house the soothing twilight ruled and I felt relieved to enter again.

I knew before I woke up. I think that in my sleep I must have registered the first minute tightening of the smallest muscle, long before it grew stronger and turned into regular cramps. The warm sticky liquid between my legs was just confirmation of the already accepted fact. There was blood down my thighs, on the sheets and on the bathrobe. I lay still and invited the pain. Each intense cramp brought with it a fresh flow of thick blood. I thought that if I allowed it space, offered no resistance, then perhaps it would not stop and we would die together.

But in the morning it was over. I stood in the shower, my teeth chattering, and watched the red water swirl into the drain. I held up my face and my tears mixed with the water.

I left New Zealand two weeks later. Erica drove me to the airport. She had asked no questions when I entered her life, and she asked none now. I had told her I was going to stay with my father in Tokyo for some time. Her slim hands rested on the wheel and she kept her eyes on the road. I looked at her profile and wondered if she was relieved I was leaving. I wondered if she associated me with her grief.

She waited while I checked in and we went upstairs and sat down for a cup of coffee. 'I hope you will come back,' she said. 'You will always be welcome.' Her eyes set on my face and remained there, her brows pulled. I tried to read her expression, and it struck me that she seemed to be memorising my face. Or perhaps she was just exploring it for the first time. Perhaps she had never stopped to look at my face properly before. Perhaps, like me, she had thought there would be so much time.

When we said goodbye and embraced, I could feel the sharp shoulderblades on her back. She felt light as air in my arms. We let go and she stood back for a moment, then pulled out an envelope from her purse. 'I want you to take this,' she said, and held it out for me. 'Open it later.' She straightened, searched my face a final time, then turned and walked away, a narrow back disappearing in the crowd.

I looked out the window as the plane ascended, but this time low clouds hid the view. I stared into the compact whiteness and my mind was blank.

Later, I opened the envelope. Inside there was a photograph and a small handwritten note:

This is my favourite picture of James. He was eight and had just had a cut in his lip stitched. Yet, as you can see, he was very happy. His rugby team had just scored its first win. I look at it often and I tell myself that there was so much happiness. So much laughter. And that this is what I must remember. I hope, Veronika, that you can do the same.

29

. . . a light that is neither hope nor faith
but love — a sign of triumph.

The sky was white and there was no wind; the air was heavy and hot. Fitting weather for a funeral, Veronika thought. She had woken early, sweaty, and after a quick shower she had taken her coffee and sat down on the front steps. Her mobile phone lay beside her on the stone slab. She had rung nobody since she arrived in the village. Four months. But she had kept it charged, and every now and then she had erased the messages that had accumulated in the inbox. Holding it now in her hand she flicked to the saved messages. There were just three, the last one dated 1 November the previous year. The first was dated 6 July. Her birthday. She looked at the date, weighed the phone in her hand, but didn't listen to the recorded message. Instead, she turned off the phone, stuck it in the pocket of her bathrobe and went inside to get ready for the day.

Astrid was sitting on the bench on her porch when Veronika walked up to the house. She wore a white shirt and navy trousers and she had a plastic carry-bag on her lap. They had decided they would walk down to the church unless it rained. Astrid rose as Veronika approached and arm in arm they strolled slowly down the hill. The sky hung heavy over their heads and the swallows flew low. They passed the shop, open but deserted. Punnets of strawberries on special were displayed on a table just outside, the sweet smell attracting insects. Crossing the river, they stopped briefly. Astrid looked down on the water below. The surface was dull and flat, like an oily skin over the dark, slow-moving mass. 'It's almost over,' she said, looking across to the church.

The undertaker met them on the church steps, together with a short blonde woman. He was dressed in a dark suit, white shirt and discreet grey tie, his colleague in a dark two-piece. He introduced the woman, then turned towards the open church door. 'Follow me into the sacristy,' he said, and held out his arm to Astrid. Veronika and the blonde woman followed. It was cool inside, but the air was stale, as if the room had been closed for a long time. The priest was young, not much older than herself, Veronika thought. He held his hands clasped as if in constant prayer, but it seemed to be a sign of nervousness rather than piety. He released one hand momentarily to greet Astrid. His eyes avoided Veronika's.

As they walked into the church, Veronika noticed three elderly women in one of the pews towards the back, otherwise the church was empty. They walked up the aisle, the priest leading, Astrid following, leaning on Veronika's arm, then the undertaker and his colleague. The coffin was a plain wooden one, and the only adornment was a small wreath of silver fir. On either side a waist-high wrought-iron candlestick held a lit candle.

Astrid sat in the front pew with Veronika by her side and the undertakers sat down behind them. The priest read the prescribed texts but made no attempt at a personal speech. To Veronika, the words seemed to disperse as soon as they left his lips, the syllables drifting apart and the meaning lost unto the dark silent spaces of the vast room. As he finished, the organ began to play, but Astrid remained seated. Her eyes were fixed on the coffin and her lips moved soundlessly. Then she put her arm on Veronika's, prompting her to rise to let the old woman pass. On her own, Astrid walked up to the coffin and stood at the foot, her back to the pews. She looked frail and small, but her posture was confident, her back straight and her shoulders broad. Her head was not bowed in prayer, but tilted slightly upwards. Her lips moved, but Veronika couldn't hear any sounds. Astrid remained motionless, apart from the continuous silent movement of her lips. Then she felt in the pocket of her trousers and seemed to remove something. Veronika saw the clasped hand and watched the old woman stretch out and place the object on the lid of the coffin. She kept her palm there for a moment, before turning and walking over to the pew where Veronika stood waiting. The two of them walked back down the aisle. As they passed the three women, Veronika could sense their eyes on their backs.

On the church steps they were joined by the priest and the two undertakers. Astrid stood a little to the side and it looked as if she was taking deep breaths of the humid air. Asked if she would attend the interment, she shook her head.

The undertaker's eyes rested briefly on the old woman's face. He held his head cocked to the side, but said nothing. Instead, he stretched out his hand and said goodbye. He and his colleague returned inside together with the priest, while Astrid and Veronika walked down the church steps. They had stepped onto the gravel and were walking towards the gate when Astrid put her hand on Veronika's arm.

'Just a moment,' she said, and turned and walked down the side of the church towards the cemetery. Veronika followed, unsure whether she should, her eyes on the old woman's back. She watched Astrid reach the far end, near the stone wall, where she awkwardly kneeled, opened the plastic bag and took out a small posy of wild flowers. She laid them on the plaque in front of her. Then she leaned forward, stroking the flat plaque with her hand, and sat immobile with her hands on her thighs. Veronika slowly walked up and offered her hand. Astrid looked up, nodded and accepted the support. She stood, brushed off her trousers and twisted the plastic bag in her hands.

'I gave back the ring,' she said. 'I should never have accepted it. And I shouldn't have left it a lifetime to say the words. But now, it is finally over.'

30

. . . mysteriously deep the moments
when pure joy is us allowed.

Thirty-one. I am thirty-one years old, Veronika thought. She was in bed; it was Saturday. It was her birthday, the sixth of July. She looked at the light washing over the ceiling. It was still early, but the breeze that filtered in through the mosquito mesh covering the window was already the same temperature as the skin of her arm. She kicked off the sheet and turned onto her side, her hands between her legs. She was naked. She tried to recall the same morning a year earlier. In another world, another life.

'Happy birthday, Veronika.' She felt his lips against her thighs underneath the blanket. She pulled it over her head and reached for his face. He kissed her lips, then gently pushed her down against the pillow and let his lips walk over her chest and stomach. As she arched to accommodate him, she was overcome by a sense of joy so intense it splintered and burst into multicoloured fragments that filled the entire universe.

Afterwards, as she lay with her head on his chest, her damp hair plastered to his skin, she said, 'It's my birthday. My first birthday. This is where my life begins.' She closed her eyes and smelled his skin. And she knew that births were like this — hot, smelly, dangerous, even life-threatening. Jubilant.

They spent the day doing all the things she had come to love. Hours in the art gallery, then browsing the little shops down High Street, stopping at her favourite bookstore, then coffee, two flat whites, which James had the waitress make sure had the milk swirled into a heart. She laughed, too, the waitress. He could make anybody laugh. It was as if even the weather did its best to make it her day. The sky was intensely blue, the air crisp, and when they sat down for lunch they picked a table out on the pavement. It was warm in the sun and James removed his jacket. He took off his sunglasses and looked intently at her.

'This is how it will always be. Whatever happens, wherever we go, we will make sure this is how it stays. Until the day we die.' He pulled a small green velvet pouch from his pocket. 'Happy birthday, Veronika,' he said and pushed it across the table.

She left it there, only stroked the soft material with her fingers. 'Remember when you gave me the mobile?' she said. 'And I gave you nothing?'

He smiled and shook his head. 'Self-interest,' he said. 'Pure self-ishness. I just needed to know I would be able to reach you.'

'Well, I have given you nothing.' She looked into his eyes, her hand still fondling the velvet pouch. 'So, I am giving you my next book. It's all for you. For James with all my love. And it will be a book of love. It will contain all this.' She made a gesture that captured the two of them, the café, the street beyond, the sky. 'And I will make it so very beautiful.' She took up the pouch and opened it. Inside was a piece of very dark, almost black greenstone. A rectangular piece, the size of a matchbox, but thinning at the middle, making the centre almost transparent. James stretched out his hand for her to place it on his palm. He lifted the stone and held it against the sun.

'Here,' he said. 'Look here. If you look with the right heart you can see the land. You can see the sea. The mountains, the skies. The people.' He opened the clasp and leaned across to place the thin cord around her neck. 'It's yours,' he said. 'It's all yours. All of this.'

A year ago. On the other side of the earth. In another life.

She opened her eyes and set them on the blind, which bounced gently in the morning breeze. It was early, but she sat up and bent over to pull out the drawer of the bedside table. She removed the small velvet pouch and opened it. The greenstone slid out and landed on her lap. She held it up against the soft light, then tied it around her neck. One hand still around the smooth stone, she took out her mobile phone. Turning it on, she placed it on the bedside table. She walked across the floor to the window, pulled up the blind and stood there looking, her hand still around the greenstone. The summer was at its peak, bursting with exuberance. The high grass was mixed with bluebells and daisies, the leaves of the birches a rich, saturated green. She could hear the swallows that were nesting above, just underneath the roof, the fledglings ready to fly any day now.

They had agreed to leave while the morning was still fresh, before the midday heat, but it was still a while before she had to start getting ready. She pulled on the red bathrobe and went downstairs to make coffee. Mug in hand, she opened the front door. On the doorstep there was a white plate with a timothy straw of small bright-red wild strawberries. Veronika sat down and took the straw in her hand. She held it up and smiled, put it close to her nose and smelled it, before slowly pulling off a berry and putting it in her mouth. She ate them all, one at a time, and let the sweetness stay on her tongue while her bare feet sat on the morning-moist grass. The distant sound of a woodpecker cut through the drowsy morning, otherwise all was still. She had come to treasure these mornings on the steps. Each was a new beginning, a clean slate. She drifted closer to the surface day by day, and the light grew.

Dressed and ready to leave, she stopped herself and went upstairs. She returned with the mobile, which she pushed into the pocket of her small backpack.

For the first time since they met, Astrid was wearing a skirt. The dark-red fine wool reached her ankles as she rose from the bench and walked towards the gate. She wore flat black shoes and a white short-sleeved blouse. Veronika noticed she wore earrings, small white pearls. She carried an old-fashioned wicker basket, the kind you would use for picking berries or mushrooms.

Veronika had booked lunch at a small pension in a neighbouring village, where the food was said to be very good. They would drive through the village on their way to the city, then return the same way and stop to eat.

'I like driving,' Veronika said. 'I never really knew that, until recently. This is the first time in my life I have had a car of my own. Though of course it isn't really mine, it's rented. But I think of it as mine. And I think of it rather like a pet. When I take it for a ride, it's like taking a dog for a walk.' She smiled and patted the steering wheel.

The road was dry and empty; the radio played popular music. They drove slowly and were overtaken a few times. Astrid took a bag of sweets from her basket and held it out for Veronika to help herself.

'In one place where I lived with my father he had a driver called Muhammad,' Veronika said. 'He was illiterate, but my father only discovered this when he wanted to let him go. The other staff petitioned on the old man's behalf when they heard. Muhammad had four adopted children, and one of them was still to finish university. Illiterate and old, Muhammad would never find a new job. When my father heard, he immediately gave in and Muhammad stayed and drove us until we left.'

Veronika had her eyes fixed on the road. She pulled her hair away from her face with her left hand. 'My father is a gentle, kind man.' She threw a quick glance at Astrid. 'I have spent more time with my father than with anybody else. Yet when I look at him now, as an adult, I am not so sure I know him. I know he is kind, I know he is gentle. I know what he likes to read, what music he enjoys, what sports. But I don't know what he thinks. I don't know him as a person. Just as my father.' Her right hand on the steering wheel moved, the fingers tapped and the hand clasped and released.

Just then the mobile rang. But the bag was in the back seat and when Astrid made an attempt at reaching for it, Veronika put her hand on the old woman's arm and shook her head. 'Let it ring,' she said. 'I'll check it later.'

They drove through drowsy villages where the rusty-red

wooden houses with white trims sat surrounded by flowerbeds and bright green lawns. They saw few people; it was still early. There were long stretches where the road ran along the river, which was wide and still, a peacefully meandering metallic waterway, reflecting the blue sky.

They reached the city just before ten and found a carpark outside the domed shopping mall. There was still a little time to go before the shops opened so they decided to take a stroll in the park across the street while they waited. When they saw the doors open they returned and went inside. Seemingly the only early shoppers, they walked slowly past shop windows where the displays looked as drowsy as the city itself. The summer clothes and holiday articles seemed a little faded, as if covered in light dust, resignedly waiting to be dismantled to make room for next season's displays.

In one shop a thin young girl with bleached straight hair stood behind the counter. She had a small mirror in her hand and was occupied applying lip-gloss with her finger. She showed no sign of having noticed the two women. Astrid walked up to the rack where an assortment of one-piece swimsuits hung listlessly. As they had expected, the choice was limited. There were three in the right size: one black, one white with appliquéd rhinestones, and one in a bright floral pattern. Astrid was looking at the rack, her face set in an expression that Veronika couldn't quite interpret, when the girl approached.

'Looking for a swimsuit for your mother?' she asked Veronika, ignoring Astrid.

'That's right,' Veronika said. The girl held out the black swimsuit, a sensible creation with low-cut legs and wide shoulder straps. It dangled on her finger, while her eyes seemed focused somewhere across the shop floor.

'Can I try this one?' Astrid said, taking the brightly coloured floral patterned suit from the rack.

'Sure,' the girl said, still not looking at her customer. 'Fitting room's over there.' She nodded in the direction of three cubicles along the wall and turned her back on them before she had finished the sentence, returning to her place behind the counter where she resumed her make-up application.

Astrid disappeared into one of the cubicles. Veronika could hear her undressing, and the curtain across the door bulged as she moved around inside the small space. Then the curtain was abruptly pulled aside and Astrid stepped out into the bright fluorescent light.

'Well, what do you think?' she said, posing with arms outstretched and one foot in front of the other. The skin of her legs was bluish white and hung loosely over her thighs. The low-cut neckline exposed the tops of her flaccid white breasts. Her hair seemed charged with static electricity and framed her pale face like a fragile halo. There was a moment of absolute silence and Veronika slowly raised her hands to her mouth. Astrid's eyes twinkled and simultaneously both women burst into uncontrollable laughter. It began as a muted giggle that rapidly escalated until tears streamed down Astrid's face as she laughed out loud. Veronika had to bend over to catch her breath and Astrid sank down onto a stool outside the fitting room.

'Wonderful,' Veronika said when she had finally recovered enough to speak. 'I think it is absolutely perfect.'

'I'll take it,' Astrid said, and returned to the fitting room. Veronika could hear her chortle behind the curtain. The girl at the counter stood immobile, her glossy lips half open.

The swimsuit in a bag, they wandered out into the summer-drowsy city. It was too early for lunch and there was nothing more either of them needed to buy. They walked aimlessly and when they passed an ice-cream kiosk they stopped and bought a cone each. They went and sat on a park bench in light shadow underneath some trees.

'You know, I have never been here before,' Astrid said. 'I am grateful to you for letting me see all this.' She lifted her hand that held the ice-cream and indicated the surroundings. 'I am taking it all in, and I am enjoying it, but I realise now, when I actually see it, that it doesn't matter that it has taken me a whole life.' She sat with her face turned towards the sun, occasionally licking the ice-cream. 'I'm sure there are extraordinary places that I will never see. But now I don't mind.' Her voice trailed off. 'This day is enough. I know now that it would have made no difference. It was never about the place.'

Veronika reached inside her blouse and pulled out the greenstone pendant. She opened the clasp, took it off and held it up against the sun.

'Here, Astrid, look,' she said. The old woman bent over and their heads touched lightly as they both looked at the stone. 'If you have the right heart you can see everything you love in here. The lakes, the forests, the sky. The entire universe.' She held out the pendant for Astrid to touch and the old woman let her fingers run over the smooth surface. 'I haven't worn it since the day James died,' Veronika said. 'Because I lost my heart. And there was nothing for me to see.' She tied it around her neck again. 'But this morning I put it on. And I think I can see it. I think I can see the beauty again.'

Astrid looked at her. 'Yes,' the old woman said. 'Yes, there is beauty. You just have to have the heart and you can see it anywhere.'

After a short stroll through the quiet streets, they returned to the car and drove off.

The pension was a substantial old wooden house, painted pale yellow, in a village where all the other buildings were the usual rust-red. It looked like a queen bee, sitting in a large mature garden at the peak of its summer abundance, surrounded by a village of reddish-brown worker bees. They parked outside the gates and walked slowly up the path to the front door. To their right there was a herb garden with rows of parsley, dill, chives and basil. Tall hollyhocks grew along the front of the main building, on either side of the front door. A large grey cat was asleep on the front steps and a wagtail fearlessly pranced on the grass just below. There was silence as they walked through the open front door and along the hallway, and they met nobody. But just as they entered the dining room a slim woman approached with a welcoming smile. Up close they could see that she was not young, but there was an appealing energetic air about her. She spoke with a slight foreign accent and this, together with her brightly hennaed hair, made her seem intriguingly out of place in this old and staid environment.

She suggested lunch inside and coffee in the garden afterwards, and Astrid and Veronika sat down at a table in the dining room. Astrid looked up at the waitress. 'It's Veronika's birthday today,' she said with a small nod.

The waitress pressed her hands together and her smile was wide and genuine. 'Ah, how wonderful! Let me serve you a birthday drink.' She turned to leave. 'On the house, of course,' she added over her shoulder.

The room was spacious and the understated furnishing made it feel even more so. The wooden tables and chairs were painted the traditional pale grey. The wooden floor was worn and scrubbed a soft pale grey too. There were no curtains, but each window had several potted geraniums on the window-sills. The overall impression was serene and ageless, a gentle backdrop for people and food that may have looked the same for hundreds of years. Initially, they were the only guests.

Veronika was depositing her backpack on the floor beside her chair when she remembered the unanswered mobile call. She pulled out the phone and called the message service. She listened to the recording and unconsciously her face softened and she smiled. 'It was my father,' she said when she had returned the phone to her bag. 'Wishing me a happy birthday.'

The waitress returned with two glasses of sparkling wine on a small tray. 'Happy birthday,' she said as she put the glasses on the table.

Astrid took her glass and held it up. 'Happy birthday, Veronika,' she said. 'I hope you will come to my house tonight for dinner. I have no present for you with me.' Veronika smiled and nodded.

There was no menu and the entrée was self-service from a small round table across the room. There was homemade rye bread, dried as well as fresh, and butter. A small juniper-wood bowl with pale brown soft whey-cheese, a bowl with fried chanterelles, a mixed salad of a variety of leaves and flower petals. Egg halves and a small bowl of whitefish roe. Two varieties of marinated herring. Small new potatoes sprinkled with dill. They helped themselves and sat down to eat.

As they finished the entrée and sat waiting for the main course, a man and a woman arrived and sat down across the room. Veronika could hear that they were speaking English: she thought they might be American.

'My father,' Veronika said, turning the glass in her hand. 'When I was a child I thought he could do anything. Take away any pain, make my world safe and comprehensible. It was always just the two of us, all alone in the world. But I never stopped to look at him. To consider the man. He was always just my father. And he allowed me to believe that the main purpose of his life was my well-being.'

'A good father,' Astrid said. 'A loving father.' She looked up. The wine had painted her cheeks pink and Veronika suddenly thought she could again see beauty in the old face. 'Parents have such formidable power. They can protect you from all the pain in the world. Or inflict the hardest pain of all. And as children we accept what we get. Perhaps we believe that anything is better than that which we all fear the most.' She looked out the window, where the hot summer air stood still. 'Loneliness. Abandonment,' she said. 'But once you accept the fact that you have always been alone, and will always be, then your perspective can begin to change. You can become aware of the small kindnesses, the little comforts. Be grateful for them. And with time you will understand that there is nothing to fear. And much to be grateful for.' She lifted her glass and drank the last mouthful. 'For me, the realisation took a lifetime. Don't let it take you that long, Veronika.'

The main course was served at the table: minced moose-meat patties with lingon berries and creamed morels. It was rich and they ate slowly, pausing to talk or just quietly resting in the kind of company that makes no demands.

Afterwards, they made their way into the garden behind the main building, where a coffee tray had been placed on one of the tables. The waitress insisted they try the chocolate cake, a house speciality, and despite both women's remonstrations, she brought a plate with one piece of dark soft cake and two spoons. And once they had tasted a spoonful each, they somehow found the space for the rest. It was early afternoon and the day was at its peak. Swallows chased insects above their heads and the air was filled with the fragrance of a large jasmine just along from where they sat.

'I am not sure how we will be able to eat again today,' Veronika said. 'I think we will have to take a swim before dinner. Try out your new swimsuit.' Astrid smiled and nodded. 'We'll make it a late supper,' she said.

Just then the mobile rang again and this time Veronika managed to reach it in time to take the call. She could feel Astrid's eyes on her face when she answered, but then the old woman turned her face towards the sun and closed her eyes. The conversation was short, but the smile lingered on Veronika's face well after she had returned the phone to her bag.

'My father again,' she said. 'Let me tell you about when I last saw him.'

31

Like a driven wave,
Dashed by fierce winds on a rock,
So am I: alone
And crushed upon the shore,
Remembering what has been.

Veronika

The week after the funeral I rang my father. I was still unable to find the words, but he knew my voice. He asked no questions. He said, 'I am here.' And then we were silent.

He met me at the airport. He stood waiting, immaculate in his grey business suit, white shirt and tasteful tie. It was early morning; he must have come straight from home.

He hugged me briefly and took my luggage trolley. No questions, no searching looks. Quiet, unhurried efficiency. 'Let's get this over with as quickly and smoothly as possible,' was the look on his face and the language of his movements. We walked through the strangely still arrivals area, where people seemed to move soundlessly, leaving no litter, no smells. We continued in silence to the carpark, deposited my luggage in the boot of his new Japanese car and drove off.

I hadn't seen my father for over a year. I looked at his profile as he manoeuvred the car out through the tollgates of the carpark. He had aged, filled out a little. The chin was less defined, the hair a little thinner on top and a touch greyer around the ears. Up on the highway, he turned on the CD player. Frank Sinatra. In spite of everything, I smiled. I looked out the window at the passing landscape. In the winter morning light it looked tranquil. A watercolour. Dormant fields and bare trees. No people, no movement. Then, as we approached the city, concrete walls began obstructing the view, and eventually we were amid a complex web of roads, intricate layers of swiftly moving traffic. 'Fly me to the moon,' on the CD player. High-rise buildings so close to the car that it felt as if we were driving through a tunnel inside them, people going about their business on either side.

My father lived in a spacious apartment on the second floor of a three-storey building. We parked in the garage underneath and took the lift up. In the hallway I recognised the small Korean chest, the framed antique map of Stockholm. I walked into the lounge, where the two red sofas stood facing each other with the chess table in between, as they had in so many other living rooms. I was in a dream where things were familiar and strange at the same time. The small guestroom was ready, the bed made up and towels laid out. A hand-drawn map of the neighbourhood sat on the small desk with an envelope on top, no doubt containing money. But my father was off to work.

After he had left, I sat on the bed, hands between my knees. Why was I here? I walked slowly through the maze-like hallway, lined with my father's books, and with earthquake stops between the top shelf and the ceiling. Everything was tidy, silent, still. In the kitchen the fridge hummed, the bench-tops were empty and clean, the stove and the sink shiny, as if never used. I went up to the window and looked out. Across the road to the left there was a small park, with mature trees lifting bare black branches towards the white sky. Straight ahead, on the other side of the narrow road, there was a low old wooden house. On its tin roof an old woman was crouching, a large black and white cat by her side. She wore a rust-coloured jacket, a white kerchief covered her hair, white gloves her hands. A sack sat between her knees. She was picking persimmons from the branches of the overhanging tree. Slowly and gracefully, she stretched out a gloved hand, folded her fingers around a bright orange globe, twisting it gently one way, then the other until it snapped loose. Continuing the fluid movement, she deposited the fruit into the sack before reaching out for another. Meanwhile the cat sat motionless, its deformed tail outstretched behind it.

I remained there, watching, and when I left the woman was still going about her work, the cat beside her.

I went into the small guest bathroom and undressed. There were mirrors along the entire length of the room on one side, and I stood in front of them, naked. I looked at myself and could see no major changes. My skin was still tanned, with my breasts and a triangle over my pubic area a contrasting white. I ran my palms over my flat stomach and felt the emptiness behind the unblemished skin. I turned around and looked into the mirror over my shoulder. My buttocks were white and a thin white line ran across my back just under my shoulder-blades. My hair had grown and fell over my shoulders. But there was no major difference, no visible sign. I turned to the mirror and put my hands on my breasts, then hugged my shoulders, closing my eyes. But there were no tears.

After my shower, I went for a walk. The map was detailed, with precise notes in my father's tidy handwriting along the margins and on the back. It outlined the way to the station, the nearby shops and restaurants, Yoyogi Park and Meiji Shrine. It explained the system for numbering houses and gave some useful phrases in Japanese. It finished with his phone numbers. He had signed it in Swedish, 'Pappa'. I walked downhill, with no particular destination in mind. The weather was clear, but the light seemed faint, as if filtered through gauze. I walked past the park and on to the shrine. There were people here, families and couples, some tourists, but mostly Japanese visitors, moving unhurriedly, stopping along the gravel road to pose for photographs.

Inside the shrine a procession of young men dressed in white, with black headgear and black clogs, crossed the courtyard and disappeared into one of the buildings. I walked up the stairs to the main shrine, where a few visitors were praying and throwing coins into the wooden container in front of them. I stood in the shade, leaning lightly against the wall, watching. An old lady was right in front of me, her hands raised in prayer, handbag dangling on her arm. A young couple stood further away, a small baby in the father's arms. I passed the counters selling religious paraphernalia and walked down to the stand with wooden prayer tablets. There must have been hundreds, hanging in layers on a large four-sided structure. Mostly, the scribbled messages were prayers for world peace, health and happiness, good exam results, babies. But some were more personal, some very moving. Some were lighter, funny or flippant, like the one that stated: *I wish that next year I will get to see Naomi in her thong.* I smiled, but I couldn't think of anything to wish for.

In the evening my father took me to a small restaurant in Shibuya. We decided to walk, as the evening was crisp and clear. In darkness the city was transformed. Where in daylight I had seen awkward modern buildings entangled in cables hanging from concrete pillars, there were now mysterious, dimly lit alleys with paper lanterns swaying lightly in front of half-open doors. The air smelled of cooking; we passed laughing young couples. At the main crossing in Shibuya we stopped and allowed the throng of people to flow past. Bodies drifted by, seamlessly, nobody bumping into anybody else, nobody even brushing against us. We walked on, surrounded on all sides by moving people. Faces, mouths that talked, laughed, exhaled cigarette smoke. Hands gesticulating, smoothing hair, closing over a match flame, holding other hands. So close we should have been able to feel the warmth of the bodies, smell the odours. But we were separate. Separate from the surrounding crowd, and also from each other. Cocooned in conjoined bubbles, bobbing along in the crowd, but not belonging. Together in an alien world, but solitary.

The restaurant was a simple okonomiyake place, hot and smelly. We were each given a bowl containing vegetables and chicken in a mixture of egg and rice flour, which my father showed me how to cook on the hotplate on the table between us. His hands moved expertly, emptying our bowls onto the greased plate, flattening the resulting mounds with a spatula, making two perfect circles. I watched, sipping cold beer. He worked with focus, turning the pancakes with an easy flick of the spatula, sprinkling them with fish flakes and seaweed. I suddenly remembered him teaching me to fish. How he would put up the oars, set me between his legs and let me hold the handle of the fishing rod as he cast, his hand over mine. His hands were soft and always warm. I watched him now, and like an attack of intense physical pain it struck me that my father would never know the man I had loved. He would never know, and this would always separate us.

He suddenly looked up at me, as if alerted. He raised his glass, waited for me to raise mine, then gently let them clink. And the pain faded.

'Let's eat,' was all he said, but his grey eyes lingered on my face for a moment.

I stayed in Tokyo almost a month. Long enough for us to settle into a daily routine. We ate dinner out every night, usually at one of the small restaurants nearby. Some days we met for lunch in town, often at the National Museum of Modern Art, where even in winter we could sit outside on a sunny day. I sometimes took the train into town, usually just to walk the streets and watch people. I went to Asakusa several times, stopping for lunch at the same small restaurant where my father had taken me the first weekend. I would sit on the floor in the dark room, surrounded by Asian artefacts, transported into a world where I had no history and no future.

One day after lunch I walked to the Tokyo Tower. I stood at the base of the mock Eiffel structure and watched the crowds, but I didn't enter. I strolled on and came by a large Buddhist temple. At the back was a terraced area with hundreds of little stone figures, many dressed in crocheted red hats and bibs and surrounded by colourful pinwheels, teddy bears and dolls. A middle-aged European woman dressed in a heavy sports jacket and walking boots was taking pictures with a long-lens camera. I stood still, watching, and after a little while she lowered her camera and turned to me.

'Mitzuko,' she said. 'It means water child. These are the children who never made the transcendence from water to human life.' She drew a wide semi-circle in the air, indicating the rows of red-capped stone figures. 'And this is their protector,' she said, pointing to a large statue of a man holding a staff in one hand and a baby on the other arm. 'Jizo, the Buddhist deity who looks after the unborn.' She looked at me with a shy smile. 'Sorry, I am sure you know all this. It's just that it moves me so. All those children. The sadness. And you know, there is no real comfort for them, in spite of Jizo. Ever. The water children play on the shore of the river that runs between this world and the other side. They build towers with pebbles, it's their penance. Guarded by a monster. For ever. And there is this terrible double guilt. The child having caused the parents such grief by not being born. And the parents having caused the child to be in eternal limbo by not giving it life. Double guilt.' She looked down, kicking the gravel with the toe of her boot. 'Sorry,' she said, and started to put her camera back into its case. She nodded goodbye and left, her steps loud on the path. I walked along the rows of mitzuko, hands in my pockets. The pinwheels whistled softly and the odd crow cawed.

The last weekend before I left, my father and I took the train to Nikko on the Saturday morning. We had booked to stay the night at a traditional Japanese inn. We got off the train in the small town itself, deposited our bags in lockers at the station and wandered uphill to the main temple area. We let ourselves drift with the crowds around us, not ambitious enough to explore anything more closely. A pale sun shone, the air was warm and dry and we removed our jackets. I walked behind my father up the steep stone steps, watching his back. He climbed slowly, panting, stopping every now and then for a little rest, yet somehow not acknowledging the need for a pause. I suddenly saw him as he would look to other people: a man approaching sixty, a little overweight, balding. Well dressed and well kept, polite and private. Was I like him? Would I come to resemble him more and more as I aged? As a child I had wanted to look like my mother, my beautiful, glamorous mother. But I had been told I looked like my father. Now, suddenly, I took comfort from the likeness. It was soothing to realise that the man in front of me was my father. That I was his daughter.

We arrived at the inn in the late afternoon. It was utterly lacking in immediate appeal. The brochures had been absolutely correct, yet at the same time absolutely inaccurate. It was our equating 'genuinely Japanese' with 'charming' that had misled us. But after our initial disappointment at the large scale of the place and the conference hotel atmosphere, we gradually began to enjoy ourselves. Our room was small and unadorned, but overlooked a peaceful garden with large trees. We installed ourselves and donned the provided yukata robes. We had booked to have a traditional bath before dinner. I found myself alone in the ladies' baths. I had no idea of the rituals, and was relieved to be left alone to manage as best I could. After washing, I slid naked into the hot water, where I sat on the ledge that ran the length of the pool, my feet floating in front of me. The water was very hot, dark and smelled of sulphur. With my body carried by the hot water, alone in the spacious room, I again felt as if I no longer existed in the real world. As if I had entered a strange space in between life and death.

Later, we were seated in our own small dining room, just the two of us. We knelt by the table side by side, with the waitress emerging now and then through the slit in the curtain, presenting us with the courses one at a time. We talked a little about my father's work and for the first time he mentioned retirement. He thought he might take early retirement, should the offer come up. Then, suddenly, he looked at me and asked if I had talked to my mother recently. After an awkward pause I told him no. It struck me that he looked disappointed.

After dinner we went up to our room. We rang room service, ordered a beer each and sat on the laid-out futons to drink them. I told him I had decided to leave at the end of the following week. I had confirmed my ticket and would fly to Stockholm on the Friday. I knew he had long since made plans to go to Bali over Christmas, and I thought he might have worried about what to do with me if I stayed on.

He nodded, but said nothing.

We turned off the lights and lay down under our duvets. I lay on my side, looking towards the window. It was still and quiet. When later I turned onto my other side I saw my father's back, the duvet pulled up so that only the top of his head was visible. His breathing was light, but occasionally there was a slight pause, a hiccup in the flow of air. I turned onto my back, and I was suddenly overcome by such sadness. A gentle, unspecific sadness, not the raw physical pain of before. I rolled over on my side and curled up. And for the first time since I had left Auckland I cried.

In the morning we checked out after breakfast and went to see the waterfalls before taking the train back to Tokyo.

On the last morning I packed, showered and dressed. I had brought a small piece of carved greenstone from New Zealand for my father and I went into his bedroom to leave it on his bedside table. As I put it down, I noticed a copy of my book sitting underneath a couple of business magazines. I picked it up, weighing it in my hands. It was worn and tattered, as if having been read and reread, thumbed and carried around. I opened it and looked at the inscription. *To my father, my fellow traveller.* I put it back, and set the small pouch with the greenstone on top.

My father had tried to insist on driving me to the airport but I had refused. The compromise was that he was coming back from the office to drive me to the bus station. I stood ready, looking out the window, watching him drive up to the front door of the building, and I was just closing the door to the apartment when he stepped out of the lift to take my bag. We had agreed to allow time for lunch after checking my luggage in at the bus depot. We sat at a small table up against a glass wall, with an atrium space on the other side. Light through a glass dome high above illuminated an arrangement of smooth granite stones and tall grass. We ordered champagne and orange juice and sat sipping, as we waited for our food.

'I wish . . .' he began, but the sentence was left unfinished and he looked through the glass and out over the stones. Then he cleared his throat and started again. 'Let me know if you need anything.' Just then the waitress arrived with our food and we started to eat.

I convinced him to leave before the bus arrived. We said

goodbye in the hotel lobby. He embraced me, then let his hand slide down my arm and take hold of my hand. He gave it a small squeeze, then abruptly let go. He turned once to wave, before disappearing around a corner.

I flew to Stockholm, still not knowing where I was going.

32

. . . now let me sing you gentle songs.

They drove home in the afternoon heat and agreed that the idea of a swim seemed a good one. After a quick change they got back in the car and left for the lake.

This time there were two cars parked at the end of the road, and they found a group of teenagers noisily splashing in the water and chasing one another on the sand. Still, once they sat down, there seemed to be enough space to allow almost complete privacy.

Astrid smiled a tight-lipped smile and removed her blouse and skirt. She stood awkwardly, showing none of her earlier confidence. The gaudy swimsuit sat uncomfortably with the expression of uncertainty, even fear, on the old woman's face. Veronika dropped her shorts and stretched out her hand.

'Come, let's get in the water,' she said, and pulled Astrid

along. They waded into the smooth, dark lake, their steps a little wobbly as they crossed the strip of pebbles before reaching the soft sand further out.

'It's all about breathing,' Veronika said. 'It's often about the simple things, isn't it? Painting and photography are first about seeing, they say. Writing is about observing. Technique is secondary. Sometimes the simple is the most difficult.' She scooped water into her hands and splashed her face. 'And swimming is about breathing. Remember to breathe.' She sank her knees, so that only her head and the tops of her shoulders were visible, and beckoned to Astrid to do the same. 'Nice, isn't it?'

Astrid nodded, her lips firmly closed.

'Turn your back towards me,' Veronika said, and Astrid did as she was told. 'Now, lean on my arm. I will hold my arm under your shoulders while you stretch out your legs.' The old woman slowly leaned back until she was resting on Veronika's arm. 'Spread your arms, look at the sky. Let the water carry you. And breathe.'

And slowly, through the surface in front of Astrid, the tip of her toes emerged, like pale mushrooms growing on the still surface. 'Ah,' she said, nothing more.

When the old woman seemed comfortable and her breathing calm, Veronika gradually loosened her hold of Astrid's shoulders, until her body was supported only by a light touch at the back of her head, then finally just the tips of Veronika's fingers.

When the old woman stood up again, she leaned over and put her cool fingers, where the skin had wrinkled, on Veronika's cheeks. 'Thank you,' she said, and waded uncertainly towards the beach. Veronika went further out and dived into the golden water.

When she walked back across the sand she found Astrid sitting in her usual fashion, legs stretched out in front of her. She wore her faded sunhat and her glasses and she was reading from a small book.

'It's been so long since I read this,' she said, holding up the book. 'Karin Boye. Sit down and let me read you this one.' She indicated the blanket and Veronika sat, hugging her shins and squinting out over the lake. 'It is called "Min stackars unge, My poor little child".' Astrid's voice trembled a little as she began to read:

> My poor child, so afraid of the dark,
> who has met ghosts of another kind,
> who always among those clad in white
> glimpses those with evil faces,
> now let me sing you gentle songs,
> from fright they free, from force and cramp.
> Of the evil they ask no repentance.
> Of the good they ask not for battle.
>
> See, you must know, that all that lives
> is deep inside of equal kind.
> Like trees and herbs it seeks to grow —
> pulled forward by its inner laws.
> And trees may fall and flowers wilt
> and branches break, their power lost,
> still the dream remains — awaits the call —
> in every living drop of sap.

She took off her glasses and closed the book. 'I have always loved it.' She let the book sink onto her lap. '"Let me sing you gentle songs." It is such a beautiful line,' she said. Veronika stretched out her hand and Astrid handed her the open book. 'I have never heard it before,' she said, her eyes on the page. She read silently for a while. 'It is. It is very beautiful.' She held the book in her hands and looked out over the lake.

They drove back with the windows open and the wind against their faces. When Veronika stopped to let Astrid off at her gate, the old woman turned and looked at her. 'I think I shall call this my birthday, too. Welcome to our joint birthday celebration tonight.' She put her hand on Veronika's for a moment, before stepping out of the car.

Veronika had showered. Dripping and naked she wiped the steam off the mirror over the hand-basin and looked at her image. It felt like a very long time since she had seen her reflection. She studied her face, the large green eyes framed by short black eyelashes and distinct black eyebrows, the long nose, the wide mouth. She wondered if she might have lost weight. Her face seemed thinner, the cheeks a little hollow. Or perhaps these were just signs of ageing. She lifted her hair and inspected her chin. She touched her breasts, weighed them in her hands, wondering if they, too, had aged. She ran her palms over the skin of her arms, her stomach, her thighs. And she could feel the softness.

She dressed in jeans and a white shirt and with a glass of white wine in her hand she went and sat on the front step. Heat still lingered in the air. She looked up at the sky, which seemed to arch infinitely above, and she knew that this was the moment when the shift occurred. Nothing had changed from the moment immediately before, yet everything had just changed irrevocably. Summer was no longer pausing: it had begun its retreat.

She could hear music through the open kitchen window as she approached Astrid's house. The intense sounds of the Brahms sonata seemed to reinforce her sense of loss. The awareness that time was finite, an end approaching. She stopped in her steps, her eyes on the window, where she could see Astrid moving in the lit kitchen, and she was overcome by a memory from her childhood. Standing outside a house, looking through the window at her parents kissing. She realised now that it was her only memory of any sign of affection between her parents. She must have been young, perhaps five, but old enough to be outside in the darkness. On her own, outside.

She entered the kitchen, where Astrid was busy by the stove. On the table there was a serving plate with thinly sliced gravlax and a small bowl with mustard sauce. A basket with dark rye bread stood to one side, and two champagne flutes next to a chilled bottle of fine French champagne. The table was again set with the delicate china and the wine glasses were crystal, decorated with a gold pattern. Astrid moved purposefully between stove and table, her red skirt flowing around her legs. She had changed her white blouse for a long-sleeved sheer jacket of cream silk. The sleeves were wide and she had pulled them up, leaving her arms bare. She noticed Veronika's look and shrugged her shoulders as if embarrassed.

'I know, it's a strange thing to wear. Not really intended for social occasions. It used to be my mother's. A sort of camisole, I suppose. But it is so very beautiful and I thought it would be appropriate for this celebration.' She smiled a little smile and turned back to the stove.

Veronika poured the champagne and they drank a toast,

letting the glasses clink lightly. While Astrid cooked, they helped themselves to slices of bread with salmon and mustard. The light from the setting sun made slanted inroads, blending with the light over the table. The candles on the table flickered in the breaths of warm wind that wafted in through the window.

'Now, let's sit down,' Astrid said, carrying a plate and a bowl across from the stove. 'It's been an eventful day for me. Filled with new experiences,' she said. 'This dish is not new to me, but I have never cooked it. And it's been a very long time since I tasted it. My mother used to make it and it was my favourite. She had a name for it, but my father just called it fish balls.'

She spread her napkin over her lap and held out the plate for Veronika to serve herself. 'I had the shop get me fresh pike,' Astrid said, putting the plate back on the table. Without serving herself, she looked expectantly at Veronika, who helped herself to new potatoes and snow peas, and then the fish balls. The old woman sat still, watching, until Veronika started to eat.

'It is delicious,' Veronika said, realising that she sounded surprised. 'Absolutely delicious.'

Astrid smiled and finally began to serve herself. She had bought New Zealand wine. Ordered at the local shop and carried back home. The vivid picture of the old woman making several trips to the shop made Veronika's throat tighten, but when she looked across at Astrid, she saw a face reflecting peace and happiness, perhaps even anticipation. Veronika relaxed, took a sip of the cool wine and let the flavours fill her mouth.

When they had finished eating they cleared the table and

Astrid went to the pantry, returning with a cut-crystal bowl half filled with wild strawberries. 'I had intended to make a cake but I ran out of time. All this swimming,' she said with a smile. 'But I rather prefer them like this, with just a little cream poured over.'

She sat down and pushed a slim package across the table. 'Your present,' she said. 'Happy birthday, Veronika.' Veronika unwrapped the package to reveal a small leather-bound book. The leather was dark brown, cracked and worn.

'It's my mother's diary,' said Astrid. 'You will find the recipe for the fish balls in there. But also so much else.' She stood and walked around the table, sitting down on the chair next to Veronika's. 'It begins like a diary. In April the year I was born. Here, look.' Astrid carefully opened the book on the first page. '*To Sara on her birthday from Tate.* It was a present from my grandfather. And you will see that it reads like a diary at first. She didn't write daily, just now and then. But here, at the beginning, it contains dated short notes about her life. It's personal and straightforward. As you read on, you will see the difference.' Astrid turned the pages slowly, her eyes scanning each one. 'I have read it so many times, each page is clear in my mind. Every word, the look of the ink on the page. I don't need it any more. But I want to see it in the hands of someone who will protect it.' She closed the book and pushed it towards Veronika, her hand still covering it. 'I can't think of a better keeper.'

Veronika was close to tears. She took the book and held it in her hands. 'Oh, Astrid.' She bent forward and placed a kiss on the old woman's forehead. 'I will keep it and I will protect it. Thank you.'

Astrid returned to her seat opposite Veronika. 'Don't read

it now. Wait until you are ready. There is no hurry,' she said. 'There will be time.'

Veronika nodded slowly.

'When I woke up this morning, I thought about my birthday a year ago,' she said. 'And I thought I would never again be able to enjoy a birthday.' She looked at Astrid and stretched out her hand across the table, reaching for the old woman's. 'But you have given me the best birthday I have ever had.'

'Remember, it's mine, too,' Astrid said, and smiled.

33

∴ . . . and he who gazes towards the stars
will never again be quite alone.

Summer had turned. Although the weather remained sunny and warm, with each morning the air grew a touch crisper, the light a shade sharper, the evenings a notch darker. The apples on the trees in Astrid's orchard were ripening, and one day Veronika helped her pick the cherries that remained after the birds had explored the old tree. There weren't enough to make jam, but in the afternoon they ate the sweet berries seated in the shade on the front porch.

After dinner one evening Veronika sat at her kitchen table. Her book was taking shape, and she was watching the path it took with growing excitement. It wasn't James's book, she knew that now. This book had intruded and she was beginning to think that this was just as it should be. She would write James's book. Just not yet.

She stood up and stretched her arms over her head while she walked towards the door. Out on the front steps she could see the bright yellow full moon smiling in the black sky just over the treetops. It was a Saturday in mid-August and she had invited Astrid for a traditional crayfish dinner. They had adopted a comfortable routine that involved daily walks and dinner once or twice a week, alternating the hosting. Life had taken on a gentle, predictable rhythm. Veronica felt at peace, resting in the present.

She was just about to sit down on the steps when she heard the mobile ring, muted sounds from upstairs, yet ripping the peace with its unexpected insistence. She ran up the wooden stairs and caught the call on its last ring. It was her father.

The moon had inched higher in the sky as Astrid arrived, carrying a bundle of small paper lanterns attached to an electric cord. 'I found these in the storeroom,' she smiled. 'I have no idea if they work. They might be dangerous to use.' But Veronika took the bundle and began to untangle the cord. She had set the table for two, with red paper napkins and the customary silly paper hats and bibs. There was a serving platter with a mountain of small freshwater crayfish topped with heads of dill. There was bread, butter and two kinds of cheese. And an iced bottle of aquavit. The laptop sat on the kitchen counter playing traditional drinking songs.

Astrid watched Veronika struggling with the cord and she reached out and took one end. Between them they managed to sort out the tangles and Veronika stepped up onto one of the chairs, tying one end of the cord to the fitting holding the window blind. Then she moved to the other side of the window and attached the other end. The string of lanterns hung in a deep bow across the window and when she plugged the cord into the wall socket all but one lit up. Astrid turned off the lamp, and with only the lanterns and the candles on the table, the room took on a different ambience. The corners disappeared into obscurity, and the table looked festive, perhaps even a little mysterious. Veronika changed the music to a CD with folk music. And they sat down to eat.

'My father rang today,' Veronika said, as they were finishing the last crayfish. Astrid looked up, still sucking on a shell. 'He rang to tell me he is coming back to Sweden to live. He has accepted an offer of early retirement. He asked if I would like to come and visit once he has settled in. And then perhaps take a holiday with him. Make another trip together.' Veronika absentmindedly pushed the crayfish shells about on her plate with her finger. 'He said he has missed me.' She had her eyes on her hands, but her mind was elsewhere. 'And I realised I have missed him, too. I have been thinking that perhaps one day I should go back to New Zealand. That perhaps I need some kind of closure.' She looked up at Astrid. 'I have been thinking that I left without finishing my life there. That I need to go back.'

Astrid wiped her fingers on a napkin. 'I think that if we just listen to ourselves we know what it is we have to do,' she said slowly. 'And I have come to think that however much it hurts, however hard it is, we have to listen. We have to live our lives.' She looked at Veronika, her head tilted a little as if she were trying to find the right words. 'You have been here half a year now. I think perhaps it is time. When you are ready. There is no hurry. But the day will come when your decision will be clear.'

She poured herself a small glass of aquavit and handed the

bottle over to Veronika. 'Let's drink,' she said, and lifted her glass. 'To you, Veronika. To your life.' She set the glass on the table and looked at Veronika, her head cocked. 'There is more to do,' she said. 'It's lingon berry time. And mushroom time. Will you come with me into the forest?' Veronika nodded and it was decided.

But the following morning Veronika woke up to the sound of rain. She looked out the window but there was no view; she could hardly see Astrid's house through the heavy downpour. It rained all day and towards the evening it shifted, as if reducing its force in order to last longer. Dressed in raincoats and boots, the two women went for their daily walk but the day in the forest had to be postponed for three days.

Then, finally, clear skies. They left it another day, to allow the ground to dry out a little. It was early and the air had not yet warmed when Veronika knocked on Astrid's door. She stood on the porch waiting, and filled her lungs with the clean air. The smell of autumn was distinct now after the rain. Wet leaves, bark. Sand and clay.

'It's not that either of us will need the jam for the winter,' Astrid had said with an odd little smile, her eyes locking with Veronika's. 'It's just that I think it is one of the nicest things to do here. And I think you should know.' She had paused, as if wanting her words to sink in before she continued. 'If the weather is good, we can take lunch. And we will visit all my secret places, where the berries grow in abundance. We may even find some mushrooms, though it's a little early.'

As Veronika took another deep breath of the glassy air, she knew it would be a perfect day. Astrid opened the door, her basket in her hand and wearing her cut-off boots. Veronika had a small backpack with their lunch. They set out across the fields and into the forest, where the semi-darkness underneath the dense firs was still and cool. The terrain sloped upwards and Astrid walked slowly. Veronika's eyes were on the old woman's back. Although her steps were slow, they seemed confident, as if she were in her own element. She seemed to find sure footing naturally and she moved with grace and purpose.

The dark forest gradually thinned as they reached higher ground. Eventually it gave way to tall pines, seemingly nourished only by the white moss that covered their roots. The trunks stretched straight and branchless towards the sky and the air was filled with a smell of resin and pine needles. The moss was dotted with the small red berries and they began to pick. The berries grew in clusters and they could sit down comfortably and pick from one spot for quite a while. Veronika focused on her task, the sun warm on her back now. When she looked up she found Astrid lying back on the moss, looking up at the sky.

'Thank you, Veronika,' she said.

Veronika smiled. 'What for?'

'Oh, for all of this,' Astrid said. 'All of it.'

Their baskets heavy with berries, they walked on and again entered the forest. Beside a large block of granite, Astrid stopped. She stretched out her hand and patted the moss that covered the stone. 'This is it. My praying stone. Where I used to stop, when I still believed that prayers mattered.' She stood still for a moment, lost in thought, her hand resting on the stone. Then they continued, Astrid leading the way through the dense forest. Veronika could see no path, and although Astrid kept holding branches aside for her to pass, they were both scratched on their arms as they pressed forward.

Then, abruptly, the forest ended. They parted the branches and stepped out into bright sunshine. And it was just as Astrid had described it. A circle surrounded by a solid wall of trees. Soft grass, silky and shiny in the sun, the colour of dry flax, sprinkled with wild strawberry plants, their leaves yellowing. It was strangely still, not a breath of wind, soothingly warm and absolutely peaceful. Above, the sky rose glassy blue and without a speck. They sat down on the grass. Veronika took a berry from her basket and let the tart freshness fill her mouth. They were both silent.

Later they unpacked their lunch, sandwiches and coffee, and ate, taking their time. The sun warmed here in the shelter of the trees and they removed their jackets and lay down on them. Veronika looked up into the achingly clear sky. The rest of the world felt distant, unreal. She closed her eyes.

Suddenly she felt Astrid's hand on her arm. 'Look,' the old woman whispered. The sun had sunk a little lower in the sky and the shadows from the trees had advanced into the clearing. Veronika's eyes followed Astrid's gaze. A large grey bird flew soundlessly across the blue circle above. An owl. Astrid put her finger across her lips and whispered a soft 'Shhhhh'. The bird swept back and forth over their heads several times before disappearing into the darkness of the trees. They sat up and Astrid turned to Veronika and smiled. 'Time to go,' she said.

On the way back, Astrid took a different route, where thick moist moss covered the ground, giving a misleading impression of softness. Underneath, there were deep crevasses and stones, and they had to watch their step. Astrid kept her eyes on the ground and when she suddenly stopped and bent down, she had found a patch almost covered in bright orange mushrooms.

'Ah, look here,' she said. 'Milkcaps, saffron milkcaps.' From her pocket she produced a small knife and began to cut off the mushrooms. 'Nobody else picks these,' she said, without looking up. When she finally stood, she had a small heap of mushrooms in her basket, on top of the dark red lingon berries. 'Look,' she said, holding up one mushroom. 'They bleed when you cut them.' She broke of a piece of the hat and drops of dark red sap collected along the edge. 'Looks like blood. Perhaps that's why people don't like them.' She returned the mushroom to the basket and wiped her fingers on her trousers. 'Appropriate for a witch, though,' she said with a little smile.

They continued and Astrid found more mushrooms and filled her basket to the rim. When they left the forest and slowly made their way over the meadows down towards the houses, the sun had sunk below the rim of treetops, colouring the sky over the village a pale pink, softened by the mist rising from the river.

'I'll clean the mushrooms and we can have mushroom omelette for dinner,' Astrid said. 'If you like,' she added with a quick look at Veronika. 'And before dinner we can clean the berries and make the jam. Let's carry the little cooker outside.' She put her basket down on the porch steps. 'I'll open the window and go and get the extension cord.'

'I'll run over and get some wine, then,' Veronika said.

While the sun set, they cleaned the berries, which ran through their fingers, dry and shiny. They had both picked cleanly and there was just the odd pine needle or small leaf to remove. When they had gone through both baskets, Astrid's large pot was half filled with berries. She added the sugar and placed the pot on the stove. The sweet smell of the boiling jam filled the air as they sat back with their wine glasses. Astrid began cleaning the mushrooms, dropping one at a time into a bowl while the scraps landed on the towel that covered her lap. She looked very comfortable, working swiftly and expertly, tossing the clean mushrooms into the bowl with a flick of her wrist.

'You were right,' Veronika said. 'It's been a perfect day.'

Astrid looked up and smiled. 'I thought you would like it.' She looked up at the sky, intensely dark blue now, with a tinge of purple. 'There is nothing quite like it. Perhaps it is a human instinct, this urge to harvest before the winter. Picking berries and mushrooms. Preserving. Preparing. I have always found it so very satisfying.' When she had finished cleaning the mushrooms she picked up the towel from her lap and stood to shake it. 'And it is my favourite season, autumn. Some see it as the end of the year. Death. But to me, it has always felt like the beginning. Pure and clean, with a lack of distractions. Time to set your house in order and prepare for winter.' She sat down again, leaning back against the wall and turning the wine glass between her stained fingers. 'And it is. My house is in order,' she said.

They stayed on the porch, and when the air grew chilly and the mist began to rise, Astrid went inside, returning with two woollen blankets. They wrapped themselves and sat comfortably in the gradually deepening darkness. Veronika looked up into the sky and as her eyes adjusted she watched the intensely blue-black void fill with stars.

34

Give a word or two
and it's easy to go.
All our meetings
should be just so.

All Saints Day. The first Saturday in November. Veronika was in the kitchen, lighting a fire in the stove. The weather had turned cold, but the last few weeks had been still and gentle. The landscape looked as if it had been softened by a kind hand, with light snow on the ground and a thin veil over the sky. There had been sun, but it sat low in the sky, pale and filtered through fog that lingered throughout the day.

Her packing was almost completed. She had arrived with little luggage and she hadn't added much, yet the process felt like a major undertaking, associated with intense and disparate feelings that she could neither fully understand, nor control.

She was driving to Stockholm the following morning to meet her father. She had made no further plans, but she had talked to him briefly about New Zealand. 'It's one of the few places I have not yet seen,' her father had said. 'I have never been to New Zealand.' He had said nothing further and she had not responded. She felt she needed more time to decide if she wanted company on the trip. And she thought he understood.

Packing, which was a process she normally dreaded and deferred to the last minute, felt different this time. Still an upheaval, a major task, yet somehow filled with purpose, even an element of anticipation. Although her plans were still not fully developed, her actions were conscious and deliberate. She was ready, and she was in charge.

Yet, here at the table with her coffee, looking out the window at Astrid's house, she was overcome by entirely different feelings. The consequences of her imminent departure suddenly surfaced in a rush. It had weighed like a distinct physical pain that she had carried with her constantly, but submerged, at the back of her mind. Going about her preparations, she had woken up with the subconscious awareness of a lingering sadness. Now she marvelled at the realisation that her mind could contain such contrasting feelings simultaneously. She realised that she had made the house and the village her home. That for the first time she was facing a departure that would be tinged with sadness.

She looked across to Astrid's house, and although she could see no sign of life, the house itself seemed alive. Slowly, she stood and went upstairs to finish packing. Her suitcase sat open on the bedroom floor, beside two boxes containing her books and CDs. She pulled out the drawer of the bedside table and picked up the few items inside: a clasp for her hair, her small notebook, a pen. And then underneath, the small diary Astrid had given her for her birthday. She sat down on the bed and opened the book. She had taken it out a couple of times before, but each time she had returned it to the drawer unopened. It had felt as if she needed more time, a different perspective, to be allowed inside the pages. Now she carefully opened it, initially not reading, just looking at the script. The handwriting was strong and driven and some pages had small drawings in the margin. There were sketches of plants and birds. Some pages seemed to have been written in several stages, as if the writer had returned to them with additional comments or second thoughts. Towards the latter part of the diary entire paragraphs were crossed out, the ink obliterating the underlying text. Veronika slowly turned back to the beginning and started to read.

> This book arrived for my birthday. I have had no mail for such a long time, but here it is, together with a letter. I don't understand why there is no mention of the child. I have written every other week, just like before. Has he not posted my letters?
>
> But they are well, both Tate and Mamele.

Veronika turned several pages.

> This girl averts her eyes now, just like all the others. It's wash day today and I can see her hanging the washing on the line. She is a sweet girl, but I know she will leave soon now.

Wash day
Beneath the high sky
my heart hangs
out to dry in the wind.

Veronika lowered the book onto her lap and looked out the window. She felt as if she could hear the words in her hands, as if somehow they reached her from the silent building outside her window.

He no longer looks at me. He locks himself in the study every evening. I have stopped painting. I stand in front of the easel, brush in my hand, but my mind is blank. It is as if I have been struck by a strange kind of blindness.

But then I walk down to the river and watch the wild gush of water rush by and the colours return. It's only there I can find them. Never inside this house.

The following couple of pages had been torn out and Veronika let her fingers run along the ragged edges of the lost paper.

I am heavy with my child, but now I wish I could somehow delay the birth. I would like to keep this child inside me. Protect it.

I think he would like it to be a son. If he gives it any thought at all. But in my heart I know it is a girl. I have decided not to ask for her to be named after my mother. I wish for her to have a name that suits this place. I wish for her to be able to live happily here. If he allows it, I will call her Astrid. The loving one.

Veronika flicked the pages over to the very last legible words.

I must make her strong. Loving, but also strong, because

There was no full stop and the remaining half-page was crossed out in ink that had obviously wet the page and made the pen rip the paper in places. Veronika closed the book and sat for a moment, looking across to the other house. Then she pulled out the red fleece jacket from her suitcase. She wrapped the soft material gently around the diary and placed the bundle underneath the top layer of clothes in the case.

When she had finished upstairs she went down to the kitchen again and sat at the table for a while. The room lay in semi-darkness as daylight was already receding, but she could see that Astrid had turned on the lamp over her kitchen table.

They had agreed to walk down to the river and then on to the church in the afternoon. On All Saints Day even those graves that were left abandoned throughout the year were likely to have a visitor. And a candle. From her childhood Veronika had a memory of visiting the grave of her grandparents on All Saints Day. She remembered a day just like the one outside her window: still, chilly and enveloped in light fog. The large cemetery in Stockholm had been lit by thousands of flickering candles. She had wandered the magical landscape, pleased to be holding her father's hand, uncertain whether her feelings of excitement were appropriate.

Veronika walked across to Astrid's. It was just after two in the afternoon, and dusk was already falling. When she knocked on the door the old woman answered quickly, fully dressed with her jacket on. She pulled her knitted hat over her hair and began to pull on her mittens as she stepped down onto the path. There was snow on the ground, but it hadn't snowed for several days and the layer on the path was worn down to the gravel. Astrid took Veronika's arm and they walked down the hill in comfortable silence.

The air was cold against their faces, but they were both dressed for the weather, Astrid in a heavy sheepskin jacket and Veronika in a padded jacket with a hood. There was no wind and they took their time, walking more slowly than they usually did on their morning walks. The trees stood bare with a thin coating of frost, and light snow covered the fields.

'The day I arrived, the weather was like this,' Veronika said. 'But there is a fundamental difference between March and November.' She looked out over the village below. There were no signs of life, other than smoke trailing from some of the chimneys, blending with the fog. 'In March, you know that if you hold on, there will be light. In November, you must have the strength to embrace darkness. Your barns should be filled, your harvest stored.' Astrid said nothing, but their steps naturally fell in rhythm. 'They say that March is the hardest month. Deaths peak in March. And I read that children born in November have the best chance, their mothers sustained by the summer. We associate spring with new life, when often it brings death.'

Veronika fell silent. When she spoke again, she stopped and turned to Astrid. 'For me, March was the hardest month,' she said. 'Spring is not for the weak, I think. But now I have had this summer, and I am ready. I am strong.' Astrid said nothing, but when they resumed their walk, her arm held Veronika's tightly.

They took the same route as on their very first walk, and as they left the small forest area and entered the open fields, they again stopped to look at the cluster of new buildings, which looked particularly forlorn in this weather. The surrounding fields lay barren and exposed, the dark clay wiped clear of snow. There were no trees, no visible growth of any kind around the houses. To Veronika, they looked to be leaning into one another for support, even more desperately than the first time they had passed them.

'I have thought about those houses,' Astrid said. 'And it made me think about many things.' They walked on. 'About how we choose to live. Look at the village and the old houses. They are clustered together. I suppose that is the very definition of a village.' They both looked across the open land towards the church.

'But they are not clinging to one another the way these new ones do,' Veronika said. 'The old houses look as if they have developed organically, over time. They don't belong together as a group — they are individual, separate houses.' They continued down the road towards the river.

'I have thought about the people who live here, in these new houses,' said Astrid. 'I think they are old people. And I don't think they are desperate at all. Or afraid.' She paused. 'I think I know what they are searching for.' Astrid lifted her head to the sky, where fog blurred the weak light of the setting sun. 'I think they came here to be with each other. I think they are people who have come to realise that they need other people. And have acted on this insight before it became too late. I hope I am right. I think it is appropriate that old people live in new houses, and young people move into the old ones.' Her hand patted Veronika's arm. 'I like to think that they are not leaning against one another because they are afraid. No, they are embracing one another. And I think it's a good thing.'

The river was moving slowly, as if the water was in the process of freezing. They walked up onto the riverbank and stood on the snow looking down at the dark undulating mass of water. There seemed to be movement underwater, but the surface was still.

'We used to skate on the river some years,' Astrid said. 'But not until January, when the ice was safe. It didn't happen every year. Sometimes, the ice never set properly.' She inhaled deeply and looked up. 'It's only November — we don't know what lies ahead for this winter.'

The road along the river to the church was still. They met no cars, heard no sounds. As they arrived at the cemetery, Veronika was surprised to be proven wrong. Very few graves had lights on them, and there was only one other visitor, an old woman lighting a candle on a grave at the far end of the cemetery.

They stopped at the Mattson family grave and Astrid pulled out four small candles from the pocket of her jacket. She bent down, placed them on the snow and lit them. It took a while — she struggled to light the match and had to light another when the first one flickered and blew out. Veronika stood back, allowing the old woman to go through with the ritual.

As Astrid stood up, panting a little, all four candles glowed on the snow. 'There was love. I think there must have been love,' she said. 'I think it's when you become convinced that it's been lost that sometimes it turns into its opposite. We must remember that our love is inside us. Always.' She felt in her pocket and pulled out a handkerchief. She blew her nose. Veronika couldn't tell whether she was crying, or whether it was just the chilly air that brought tears to the old woman's eyes.

They turned and walked over to the wall. Astrid pulled out another candle and bent down. Veronika kneeled beside her. The small plaque was covered with a thin layer of snow and they both brushed it clean with their mittened hands.

'You know, Veronika, there was a time when I was afraid to come here. Now I understand that it was my own company I feared.' She pulled off her mittens, placed the small candle on the plaque and lit it. For a little while she held her hands around the flame. 'Now I am not afraid,' she said, and pulled on her mittens again.

They walked back and, although it was still not late, the light was fading quickly. 'Come over when you are ready,' Astrid said as she opened her gate. 'I'll be waiting.'

Veronika wandered through the house. Already, it seemed to be withdrawing. It felt distant, silent. She had cleaned the entire house and returned everything to its original place. And suddenly it was no longer hers. The link between her and the house was broken. They were both looking to the next phase. She hadn't turned on the lights and when she walked up to the kitchen window she could see the warm lights in Astrid's kitchen through the darkness. She stood for a long time looking out, watching the old woman moving inside the light, a doll in a doll's house.

When she appeared on Astrid's doorstep it had started to snow. Fine dry flakes drifted sparsely overhead but seemed to disperse before reaching the ground. Inside the kitchen the table was again set for two with Astrid's fine china.

'There are rules for this dinner,' the old woman said as

she led Veronika into the kitchen. 'No farewells. This is just an ordinary dinner.' She walked over to the stove and bent down to pick up a piece of firewood. 'You'll see that the food certainly is very ordinary. Pancakes.' She smiled and turned her back to Veronika to place the firewood in the stove. 'And tomorrow, just wave as you pass,' she added without looking up. 'Don't stop.'

Veronika looked at the old woman's back. 'Agreed,' she said. 'We'll just have an ordinary dinner. Though I doubt that pancakes will ever be ordinary for me again.'

Astrid poured batter into the frying pan and Veronika poured them each a glass of red wine. She intended to place Astrid's on the side of the stove, but the old woman stretched out her hand and took the glass. 'To you, Veronika,' she said, and raised it. '*Lycklig resa.* Bon voyage.' She blushed and grimaced. 'Here I go, straight away. Full of farewells.' She put the glass down, walked up to Veronika and opened her arms. 'I might as well do it properly, then,' she said, and embraced the young woman. She held her tightly for quite some time, before releasing her hold and abruptly turning back to the stove.

After dinner they sat at the table listening to music. Astrid had played the Brahms only once. 'Once is enough for an ordinary dinner. Now let's play something else,' she said, and inserted one of Veronika's CDs. She had turned off the lamp over the table and candles provided the only light, reaching no further than their faces.

'Let me help you clean up,' Veronika said, but the old woman raised her hand and shook her head. 'I have all the time in the world to clean up,' she said. Catching herself, she again grimaced. 'This is too hard, Veronika,' she said. 'I think perhaps I will have to ask you to leave.' She looked intently at the young woman, who nodded slowly.

'Promise me you will stand there, just inside your window tomorrow,' Veronika said. 'Promise me you will return my wave.'

Astrid smiled a thin smile and nodded. 'I promise,' she said.

Veronika stood and pushed her chair back. She walked around the table and put her hands on the old woman's cheeks, pushing the hair away and tucking it behind her ears. She placed her lips on Astrid's forehead and kissed her. Then she turned and crossed the room without looking back, closing the door softly behind her.

She walked slowly down the path to the gate, then onto the road, where the light new snow lifted with each step. As she turned into her own front yard she looked back to the other house. The kitchen lay dark. She lifted her arm and waved. She couldn't be sure that there was a response, but she liked to think there was.

As Veronika closed the door, Astrid blew out the candles and sat in darkness. Although tears fell, there was a smile on her face. She looked out the window and saw Veronika outlined against the new snow. And as the young woman raised her hand and waved, Astrid raised hers.

35

. . . as the day breaks.

The road ran along a sandy stretch of land, a natural pier cutting through the water. The banks were covered in white moss, with pines stretching their tall straight trunks towards the pale sky.

It was March. Just like the first time. But the evening was clear and mild and the light soft as the sun lingered near the tree-tops, reflecting on the dark surface of the lake. Spring was early: there was no icc on the lake and though there was still snow on the fields either side of the road, the road itself stretched before her, a dry meandering strip, into the distance.

There was no other traffic: she hadn't seen a car since Ludvika. The rented Volvo was comfortable and anonymous, with the artificial smell of a new vehicle not yet tainted by contact with human bodies. Veronika had the radio tuned into a local station, the evening news and the weather forecast. She listened to the sounds more than the content — the rhythm of the language, familiar and strange at the same time. As if no longer entirely hers. She hadn't planned for such a late start, but now she was enjoying the early evening drive and the thought of staying the night. She would stop in the neighbouring village to pick up the keys from the man who was managing the estate.

Just before she left the forest behind and reached the bridge she saw two moose standing absolutely still in a small clearing. The sun had dipped behind the trees and the animals were black silhouettes against the patches of snow and last year's pale grass. She slowed down. As she crossed the bridge she could hear the muted rumbling of the river surging beneath, and to her right she could see the water swirling in deceptive slow motion.

She had been given a good description of the house and found it easily. It was a modern brick building set among older wooden houses painted the traditional rusty red. The air was still; ashen pillars of smoke rose from the chimneys. There were no sounds until a very old golden retriever beside the front steps spotted her and barked unconvincingly. She walked up the path to the front door in the approaching evening chill. The fields beyond lay black and barren, awaiting harrowing.

It was Saturday evening, and she felt a little guilty disturbing the peace as she rang the doorbell. She could hear the muffled sound of a TV through the door, and saw flickering lights in the windows of several of the other houses.

The woman who opened the door greeted her warmly and beckoned her into the hallway. Inside, the heavily furnished space was warm and cosy, with the smell of dinner still lingering.

'You must be Veronika Bergman,' the woman said, holding out her hand. She was plump and not very tall, dressed in a navy tracksuit and with large sheepskin slippers on her feet. She offered coffee, which Veronika declined, then called her husband, who emerged instantly through the doorway at the far end of the hall, as if he had been awaiting his cue. He was a big man, tall and heavy, with an open friendly face. Like his wife he was dressed in a tracksuit, the trousers tight on his muscled thighs and the top stretched over his shoulders. The sleeves were pulled up, leaving his wrists exposed. He took her hand in a firm grip, his hand rough and callused. Then he put his hands in the pockets of his tracksuit pants, and cleared his throat.

'I have made the arrangements as per instructions,' he said. 'I trust you will find it all in good order. I am pleased the weather is mild. You should have no problems with the water.' He paused, as if searching his mind for something more to say. 'Sad the way she went, the old lady. But then, it was her choice, I suppose.' He rubbed his chin with his hand and cleared his throat. 'Just a moment, I'll get the keys for you.'

He disappeared through the door to the left, and returned a moment later with a large brown envelope. He handed it over and crossed his arms. 'There are some papers for you regarding the property in there. Have a look at them when you have time and let me know if you have any questions.' He stretched out his hand to say goodbye. 'Ah. And there is a letter from Mrs Mattson in there, too. She gave instructions for me to hand it over together with the keys.' He dropped Veronika's hand and returned his to his pocket, then lowered his eyes for a moment, shifting his weight from toes to heels and back again. In the end all he said was, 'Good luck, then.'

His wife joined him in the doorway and they both waved goodbye as Veronika thanked them and stepped down the stairs. She heard the door close behind her and could sense that they were pleased to be able to resume their Saturday evening. She felt relieved, too.

Outside the gate she stopped, opened the envelope and pulled out the keys. She weighed them in her hand. There were two: one old, heavy and blackened; the other a shiny modern patent key. They sat together on a simple ring. Veronika stuck them in her pocket and got back in the car.

She started the short drive to the house. Her house.

But first, there was one more visit to make.

Dusk fell during the short drive. Bright yellow squares of light indicated the presence of the odd farmhouse along the road, but she met only a couple of cars. She slowed down at the bend just before the church came into view, then took the left turn off the main road and eventually stopped outside the looming white building. She took a deep breath. The air was cool now, with a hint of burning firewood. It was still, and all she could hear was the distant drone of the odd passing car. She walked along the western side of the church to the cemetery at the back. It was almost dark, but the snow that had survived in the shade near the wall seemed to fluoresce, giving off a pale light, and her eyes adjusted quickly.

Few of the graves looked well kept and only one or two showed signs of recent visits. Only one was new.

'When I leave this house, it will be for the cemetery. I have chosen the space, and it is paid for. I needed to make sure

I would have my own space there, you see,' Astrid had said when they passed the church one day.

And here it was, Astrid's space. A small granite plaque lying flat on the ground, no proper headstone. Just her name, and the words:

. . . nu vill jag sjunga dig milda sånger.

Beside it lay another plaque, the same size and colour, but aged, and with the name Sara only just legible underneath moss and lichen.

Veronika reached into her pocket and pulled out two pieces of New Zealand greenstone. She held them in her palm, closing her fingers around the shapes. They were smooth and warm. She placed one on each plaque. She squatted and let her fingers trace the words of the single line in the new granite.

. . . nu vill jag sjunga dig milda sånger.

Now let me sing you gentle songs.

She remained there, eventually dropping to her knees, running her hand over the cold surface in front of her.

The sudden distant barking of a dog pulled her back, and she stood slowly and made her way back to the car.

She drove past the shop, closed now, and with frayed billboards announcing special offers to no eyes. She took the last sharp turn off the road and up the steep hill. There were no lights on in any of the houses along the road. At the crest of the hill she turned left onto the unsealed road, past the fence with the row of mailboxes. The small timber sheds behind were just shadows.

She stopped outside the gate and got out. The soft hum from the cooling car motor was the only sound. She could smell last year's leaves and wet soil in the process of freezing yet another night. She paused for a moment and looked at the silent house in front of her, then opened the gate and walked up the path. The gravel was frozen solid, hard and dry under her feet. The keys bounced against her thigh as she stepped up onto the porch, and when she fished them out they were warm to the touch. She put the old key in the top lock, but it wouldn't turn and she had to press her shoulder against the door and pull the handle upwards before the lock reluctantly yielded. The patent key opened the lower lock silently at the first attempt.

She had expected the air inside the dark hallway to be stale and chilly, but instead she stepped into semi-darkness that was warm against her face: unscented, dry and comforting. It was as if the house had been waiting for her. It had been cleaned, aired and heated. It was ready. She stretched out her hand to switch on the lights, but changed her mind and continued on in darkness. She walked slowly along the hallway, her hands outstretched like a sleepwalker's, but as she entered the kitchen the pale light from the window was enough for her to find her way around. She stood by the window and looked out over the field where the grass lay flat, covered with a thin patchy layer of icy snow. She put her palms on the cold glass and pressed her forehead against it.

Her old house sat silently across the field, its black windows staring back at her without recognition. There was a child's swing set on the front lawn and the hedge along the road had been trimmed. It was no longer an orphan house.

She sat down at the kitchen table and placed the envelope in front of her. She pulled out the papers, then lifted the envelope and tipped it upside down. The letter fell out onto the tablecloth. A thick envelope, the paper yellowed and the glue so dried that a strip of sellotape had been added to keep the flap down.

It had her name on it, and the familiar handwriting was elegant, although a little uncertain: *Till min käraste Veronika.* To my beloved Veronika.

Veronika's hands smoothed the envelope and she felt a small lump inside. She shook it gently and a small object slid out, landing on the table with a soft thud. Astrid's gold pendant. Veronika picked it up and the fine chain fell between her fingers. It was a small oval locket with a star engraved on the face. She threaded the chain between her fingers, closed her hand around the pendant and rested both hands on the envelope. She looked out the window.

Then her hands searched the edge of the table and found the handles of the cutlery drawer where she knew Astrid kept her candles. She collected the brass candlestick from the mantelpiece above the stove and the box of matches from their place on top of the firewood in the basket on the floor. She lit the candle and began to read.

36

Let a good wind blow.
Let white snow fall.

Västra Sångeby January 2004

My dearest Veronika

You sit at the kitchen table. It is March again. A night
like the one when you first arrived. You have lit a candle
and I can see your hands on the table, holding this paper.
Your face is clear, your shoulders relaxed. Your hair is
falling freely in all its curly abundance, but I think you are
unconsciously pushing it away from your face, gathering it
at the nape of your neck.

But I could be completely wrong, of course. These
words may never be read. Or you could be anywhere
in the world when my letter reaches you. But if all goes

to plan, you will be here. In the kitchen where it all began. There are candles in the drawer underneath the table. Matches on top of the firewood by the stove. You should have found the house tidy, but stripped to the bare necessities. I don't want it to impose on you. Make demands. I wish for it to be a gift with no ties.

That first evening in March I was right where I place you now. By the window. I think of it now as the first spring sunshine on the ice of a lake frozen solid. It seems to me that ice somehow thaws from underneath. The warmth comes from above, but it is only when the depths below have warmed that the ice finally recedes. It grows porous, water begins to seep through, it loses its grip on the shores. Watching you arrive was that first light after such a long darkness. I watched the outline of your slight figure in the tunnel of light made by the headlights of your car until you were finished unloading. I stayed by the window long after you had closed the door. I watched the lights go out, one after another. And I think I knew that life had returned.

You have known me as no other person has. And I like to think that I have known you a little. There was a long time when I took comfort from having nothing. Nobody. But now I know that we are not meant to live like that. I am not sad that my insight came so late. I am grateful that it came at all. To some, my life may seem tragic. Wasted. That is not how it appears to me. You have given me a new perspective. You pulled me out into the bright life again, opened my eyes. Made the ice thaw. And I am so very grateful.

Love comes to us with no forewarning, and once given to us it can never be taken away. We must remember that. It can never be lost. Love is not measurable. It cannot be counted in years, minutes or seconds, kilos or grams. It cannot be quantified in any way. Nor can it be compared, one with the other. It simply is. The briefest brush with real love can sustain you for a lifetime. We must always remember that.

Don't grieve for me, Veronika. Do you remember how I said that it is sad when we forget the faces of those we love? I now think that we never do. I think that we imagine that they are lost, when what has happened is that they have become a part of us and can no longer be explored objectively. I would like you to think of me like that. Knowing that I will always be with you, though you may not be able to recall my face.

My dearest Veronika, with this house come no tasks, no musts. You are free to deal with it as you like — give it away, abandon it, sell it. But I hope that you will choose to accept it. It is a house in need of love and happiness. Deserving of it. I somehow think its time has come. Whether with you — as I hope — or someone else is not so important. I like to think that there will be children running up and down the stairs. I imagine it full of people for Christmas, New Year and midsummer. I think of leisurely summer days with children playing in the garden, picking the wild strawberries.

But then, more than the house, I think of you. This is the second time in my life that I have initiated a separation from someone I love. But this is so very different from that first time. Not sad in the normal sense of the word. I am long overdue to leave. And I like to think that you are ready to face life.

Live, Veronika! Take risks! That is really what life is about. We must pursue our own happiness. Nobody has ever lived our lives; there are no guidelines. Trust your instincts. Accept nothing but the best. But then also look for it carefully. Don't allow it to slip between your fingers. Sometimes, good things come to us in such a quiet fashion. And nothing comes complete. It is what we make of whatever we encounter that determines the outcome. What we choose to see, what we choose to save. And what we choose to remember. Never forget that all the love in your life is there, inside you, always. It can never be taken from you.

I would like you to think of me with a smile. Remember, there was love. It was just that I had allowed hatred to block the memories. Now, I think that my life ends in a triumph of sorts. I have retrieved the love of my life.

My dearest Veronika, it is all your doing. You arrived that dark March evening and you fundamentally changed my life. I can't begin to tell you how grateful I am. This house is but a small, inadequate — and potentially perhaps demanding — token of my heartfelt gratitude.

You gave me this CD player and I am playing Brahms again. The sonata for violin and piano, which my mother used to play. That also you returned to me. The music. There was silence, such a very long silence. Then you entered my life and brought it back. It has been heartbreaking, but also so very wonderful. I can't think of a more beautiful piece of music than this sonata. I listen to the second movement, and though I must admit that tears blur my vision, they are not sad tears. They are soothing, warm on my cheeks. I look out the window. It is a clear day, early afternoon with a warm slanted light on the snow. It is still and I can see the smoke from the chimneys of the houses down below in the village. Soft grey pencil lines against the intensely blue sky, where the approaching evening is already deepening the colour by the minute. This, too, is your gift to me. The ability to take in the view. To see the beauty. And it is so very beautiful.

I am happy, Veronika. Very happy. And so very, very grateful.

I would like you to take the time to get to know the house. I somehow think that you can bring to it what you brought to me. Life. I also think that perhaps the house can give you what you seem to be searching for. A home. That whether you choose to make it your home, or just your quiet refuge from time to time, it will give you a place to call home. A place to leave from, and to return to. Whatever you decide, Veronika, it must be for you. Not for me, or anybody else.

Do you remember that day by the lake, reading Karin Boye? There is a poem by her called 'Morning' that I find so very beautiful. The last lines are:

> . . . for the day is you,
> and the light is you,

243

the sun is you,
and all the beautiful, beautiful
awaiting life is you.

Now blow out the candle and go to bed. Sleep well, my
dear Veronika, and wake up to the new day tomorrow.

your
Astrid

37

. . . and all the beautiful, beautiful
awaiting life is you.

Veronika smiled when she realised she had absentmindedly gathered her hair, pulled it away from her face. But tears were falling from her chin onto the table.

'Astrid, I have finished the book,' she whispered. 'I hope you will like it, because it is your book. I came here with a bag of sorrows and a book to write. You helped me see that the sorrows were also love, joy and laughter, to be carried lightly and for ever. The book ended up being very different from the one I had in mind, but it is written, and I have it with me today, in my suitcase. I wish you were here at the other side of the table, with your coffee mug between your hands, ready to hear me read to you. Giving your approval with small nods of your head. But I think you know. And I think you approve.

'There was a sense of urgency to your story. A matter of completing something that began long ago. Healing something that had been hurting for such a long time. So, here it is, your book, Astrid. I have called it *Let me sing you gentle songs.*'

The candle spluttered and went out. Initially the room seemed very dark, but as her eyes adjusted, the light from a nearly full moon shone on the snow outside and a frail white light reflected into the room.

It was time to go to bed.

Good night — good sleep I wish for you,
my fellow wanderers.
We stop our song and part our ways — so what
if we never meet again.
I have told you a little and poorly of that
which has burnt in me and so soon will burn out,
but what love that was there, no corruption knows —
good night — good sleep to you.

DAN ANDERSSON, 'Epilog' (Epilogue) in
Efterlämnade dikter (*Posthumous poems*), 1920

Author's note

Astrid and Veronika is the tangible result of my acceptance to the inaugural postgraduate course Writing the Novel at the University of Auckland. Without the course, the book would probably never have been contemplated. Without the constructive criticism, constant encouragement and professional advice of my two tutors, Witi Ihimaera and Stephanie Johnson, it most certainly would not have been completed. I am deeply grateful to them both.

I have written in my study, which overlooks the skyline of Auckland city, where the dramatic shifts in light constantly threaten to distract. Yet, the process of writing this book has taken me to the other side of the world; in fact, as far away as it is possible to travel without turning back again. My native country has filled my mind with unprecedented intensity. But this book could not have been written anywhere but here, in New Zealand. The distance was essential.

Many have supported and encouraged my writing: tutors, fellow writers and friends. I thank you all, and especially

Linda Grey-Hughes, who set me on track and insisted I could do it. To my editor Rachel Scott — my sincere gratitude. She approached my manuscript with all the best qualities of a good editor: interest, sensitivity, thoroughness, patience, respect — and a good sense of humour. This book belongs to her too. To my friend and fellow writer Lisa M. Skoog de Lamas a special greeting, wishing her a continuous and complete recovery, and a speedy return to writing. I have missed the benefit of her critical eye and total honesty in the process of writing this book.

Finally, my love to my husband Frank, who gave me the space and the time.

Linda Olsson
Auckland, September 2005

Sources of poetry cited in the text

I am grateful to the following individuals and organisations for the permission to quote from poems and song lyrics. I have been deeply moved by the generosity, trust and kindness extended to me. My special thanks to Mats Boye, whose early unconditional permission to quote extensively from Karin Boye's poems and to include my own translations set me out with confidence on the pursuit of all the other permissions.

Fleur Adcock; Rolf Almer on behalf of the estate of Bo Bergman; Monika Kempe on behalf of the estate of Erik Blomberg; Mats Boye for quotes from Karin Boye's poems; Brita Edfelt for the verse from the poem 'Demaskering' (Unmasking) by Johannes Edfelt; the Administration of Literary Rights in Sweden (ALIS), for the licence to use lines from the poem 'Grekland' (Greece) by Gunnar Ekelöf; Professor Erik Allardt for the lines from the poem 'Ljust i mörkt' (Lights in darkness) by Ragnar Ekelund; Aina Enckell for the permission to use lines from the poem 'Bäst bygges' (Best you build) by Rabbe Enckell; Gösta Friberg;

Lars Grundström for the lines from the poem 'Må –' (May –) by Helmer Grundström; Susanna Gulin for lines from the poem 'Skuggan i rummet' (The shadow in the room) by Åke Gulin; the Hjalmar Gullberg & Greta Thott Trust Fund for permission to use lines from two poems by Hjalmar Gullberg: 'Lägg din hand i min om du har lust!' (Put your hand in mine if you so wish!) and 'Människors möte' (Human encounter); Erland Hemmer and Marie Louise Hemmer for permission to use a line from Jarl Hemmer's poem 'Stilla kväll' (Still evening); Bengt Lagerkvist for permission to use lines from Pär Lagerkvist's poems 'Vem spelar i natten?' (Who plays in the night?) and 'Solig stig är full av under' (Sunny path is full of wonder); Ehrlingförlagen AB for permission to use a verse from the song 'Visa vid midsommartid' (Song at midsummer time) by Rune Lindström; Finlands svenska författareförening (Society of Swedish Authors in Finland) for permission to use lines from Arvid Mörne's poem 'Ensam under fästet' (Alone beneath the firmament) and lines from the poem 'Jag var ett speglande vatten' (I was a reflecting water) by Emil Zilliacus; Margaret Orbell for permission to use lines from her translation of the poem 'Mātai rore au' (Love song) attributed to an unknown Maori tribe; Stiftelsen Övralid (The Övralid Trust) for the permission to use lines from Verner von Heidenstam's poem 'Månljuset' (The moonlight); Notfabriken Music Publishing AB for the licence to use one verse from the song 'Veronica', lyrics and music by Cornelis Vreewijk, copyright © 1968 Multitone AB, by Warner/Chappell Music Scandinavia AB, printed with permission from Notfabriken Music Publishing AB.

All translations by Linda Olsson unless otherwise stated. The translations make no attempt at conveying the poetic quality of the original work, but are here to give an idea of content only.

Epigraph

Bo Bergman, 'Sömnlös' (Sleepless) in *Äventyret (The adventure)*
1969. Reprinted in Vera Almer and Sven Lindner (eds), *Bo
Bergman: Dikter* 1903–69, Albert Bonniers Förlag, Stockholm,
1986, p. 168.

Chapter 1

Cornelis Vreeswijk, 'Veronica' from the album *Tio vackra visor
och personliga Persson,* Metronome MLP 15313, 1968.

Chapter 2

Emil Zilliacus, 'Jag var ett speglande vatten' (I was a reflecting
water) in *Vandring (Wanderings),* 1938. Reprinted in Tage
Nilsson and Daniel Andreae (eds), *Lyrikboken, a Swedish
anthology,* 4th ed., Bokförlaget Forum AB, Stockholm, 1983,
p. 765. (Hereafter Nilsson and Andreae.)

Chapter 3

Erik Johan Stagnelius, 'Vän i förödelsens stund' (A friend in the
moment of devastation), approx. 1818. Reprinted in Nilsson
and Andreae, p. 634.

Chapter 4

Hjalmar Gullberg, 'Lägg din hand i min om du har lust!'
(Put your hand in mine if you so wish!) in *Sonat (Sonata).*
Reprinted in *Hjalmar Gullberg dikter,* Månpocket, Stockholm,
1986, p. 76.

Chapter 5

Edith Södergran, 'Min framtid' (My future) in *Landet som icke
är (The land that is not),* 1925. Reprinted in *Edith Södergran
samlade dikter,* Månpocket, Stockholm, 2002, p. 307.

Chapter 6

Gunnar Ekelöf, 'Grekland' (Greece) in *Partitur (Score)*, 1969.
   Reprinted in Nilsson and Andreae, p.204.

Chapter 7

Arvid Mörne, 'Ensam under fästet' (Alone beneath the
   firmament) in *Vandringen och vägen (The walk and the road)*,
   1924. Reprinted in Nilsson and Andreae, p. 59.

Chapter 8

Edith Södergran, 'Sorger' (Sorrows) in *Dikter (Poems)*, 1916.
   Reprinted in *Edith Södergran samlade dikter*, Månpocket,
   Stockholm, 2002, p. 511.

Chapter 9

Jarl Hemmer, 'Stilla kväll' (Still evening) in *Väntan (Waiting)*,
   1922. Reprinted in Nilsson and Andreae, p. 347.

Erik Axel Karlfeldt, 'Jungfru Maria' (Virgin Mary) in *Fridolins
   lustgård och dalmålningar på rim (Fridolin's pavilion and
   rhymed dalecarlia paintings)*. Reprinted in Nilsson and
   Andreae, p. 379–80

'Limu, limu, lima', Swedish folksong, anonymous.

Chapter 10

Edith Södergran, 'Triumfen att finnas till' (The triumph of
   being) in *Septemberlyran (September lyre)*, 1918. Reprinted in
   Nilsson and Andreae, p. 669–70.

Chapter 11

Bo Bergman, 'Hjärtat' (The heart) in *En människa (One human
   being)*, 1908. Reprinted in Nilsson and Andreae, p. 95.

Chapter 12

Ragnar Ekelund, 'Du är hos mig . . .' (You are with me . . .) in *Ljust i mörkt (Lights in darkness)*, 1941. Reprinted in Nilsson and Andreae, p. 175.

Chapter 13

Erik Blomberg, 'Var inte rädd för mörkret' (Do not fear the darkness) in *Jorden (The earth)*, 1920. Reprinted in Nilsson and Andreae, p. 111.

Chapter 14

Dan Andersson, 'Hemlös' (Homeless) in *Svarta ballader (Black ballads)*, 1917. Reprinted in *Dan Andersson samlade dikter,* Wahlström & Widstrand, Stockholm, 1989.

Chapter 15

Johannes Edfelt, 'Demaskering' (Unmasking) in *Högmässa (Morning service)*, 1934. Reprinted in Nilsson and Andreae, p. 163.

Chapter 16

Gustaf Fröding, 'Strövtåg i hembygden' (Strolls in my neighbourhood) in *Stänk och flikar (Drops and patches)*, 1895. Reprinted in Nilsson and Andreae, p. 264.

Chapter 17

Gösta Friberg, 'Ingen' (Nobody) in *Växandet (Growth)*, 1976. Reprinted in Nilsson and Andreae, p. 256.

Chapter 18

Pär Lagerkvist, 'Vem spelar i natten?' (Who plays in the night?) in *Kaos (Chaos)*, 1919. Reprinted in Nilsson and Andreae, p. 256.

Chapter 19

Johan Ludvig Runeberg, 'Minnet' (The memory) in *Dikter. Tredje häftet (Poems. Third volume)*, 1843. Reprinted in Nilsson and Andreae, p. 552.

Chapter 20

Karin Boye, 'Tillägnan' (Dedication) in *Härdarna* (The hearths), 1927, www.karinboye.se

Chapter 21

Rune Lindström, 'Visa vid midsommartid' (Song at midsummer time), AB Nordiska Musikförlaget, Stockholm, 1946.

Chapter 22

Karin Boye, 'Morgon' (Morning) in *Moln (Clouds)*, 1922, www.karinboye.se

Chapter 23

Verner von Heidenstam, *Månljuset* (The moonlight) in *Nya dikter (New poems)*, 1915. Reprinted in Nilsson and Andreae, p. 340.

Chapter 24

Karin Boye, 'Du är min renaste tröst' (You are my purest comfort) in *Moln (Clouds)*, 1922, www.karinboye.se

Chapter 25

Åke Gulin, 'Skuggan i rummet' (The shadow in the room) in
Kattguld (Tinsel), 1970. Reprinted in Nilsson and Andreae,
p. 291.

Chapter 26

Fleur Adcock, 'Night-Piece'. Reprinted in Ian Wedde and
Harvey McQueen (eds), *The Penguin book of New Zealand
verse,* Penguin, Auckland, 1985, p. 386.

Chapter 27

Dan Andersson, 'Den hemlöse' (The homeless) in *Efterlämnade
dikter (Posthumous poems),* 1915. Reprinted in *Dan Andersson
samlade dikter,* Wahlström & Widstrand, Stockholm, 1989.

Chapter 28

Unknown Maori tribe, 'Mātai rore au' (Love song),
trans. Margaret Orbell. Reprinted in Ian Wedde and Harvey
McQueen (eds), *The Penguin book of New Zealand verse,*
Penguin, Auckland, 1985, p. 69.

Chapter 29

Rabbe Enckell, 'Bäst bygges' (Best you build) in *Sett och
återbördat (Seen and returned),* 1950. Reprinted in Nilsson and
Andreae, p. 219.

Chapter 30

Pär Lagerkvist, 'Solig stig är full av under' (Sunny path is full of
wonder) in *Genius (Genius),* 1937. Reprinted in Nilsson and
Andreae, p. 418.

Chapter 31

Minamoto no Shigeyuki, 960?–1000.

Chapter 32

Karin Boye, 'Stackars unge' (Poor little child) in *De sju dödssynderna (The Seven Deadly Sins)*, 1941, www.karinboye.se

Chapter 33

Bo Bergman, 'Stjärnornas hjälp' (Help from the stars) in *Kedjan* (The chain), 1966. Reprinted in Vera Almer and Sven Lindner (eds), *Bo Bergman: Dikter 1903–69*, Albert Bonniers Förlag, Stockholm, 1986, p. 168.

Chapter 34

Hjalmar Gullberg, 'Människors möte' (Human encounter) in *Att övervinna världen (To conquer the world)*, 1937. Reprinted in *Hjalmar Gullberg dikter*, Månpocket, Stockholm, 1986, p. 236.

Chapter 35

Cornelis Vreeswijk, 'Veronica' from the album *Tio vackra visor och personliga Persson*, Metronome MLP 15313, 1968.

Chapter 36

Helmer Grundström, 'Må —' (May–) in *Prasslet i asparnas skog* (The rustling in the aspen forest), 1954. Reprinted in Nilsson and Andreae, p. 290.

Chapter 37

Karin Boye, 'Morgon' (Morning) in *Moln (Clouds)*, 1922, www.karinboye.se

Epilogue

Dan Andersson, 'Epilog' (Epilogue) in *Efterlämnade dikter* (Posthumous poems), 1920. Reprinted in *Dan Andersson samlade dikter,* Wahlström & Widstrand, Stockholm, 1989.

A PENGUIN READERS GUIDE TO

ASTRID
&
VERONIKA

Linda Olsson

AN INTRODUCTION TO
Astrid & Veronika

It is a freezing night in March when Veronika Bergman arrives from New Zealand at her rented house north of Stockholm. Bereft after the recent death of her fiancé, Veronika is looking for a place to recover. The house is unwelcoming and unfamiliar, but as the days progress she begins to make it her own. She quickly establishes a routine of rising early, turning on her laptop to work on her novel—though the screen remains blank—and taking morning walks in the chilly, bleak grayness, until finally spring arrives, and with it, a life-changing encounter.

Astrid Mattson lives in the only house next door and is often described as "the neighborhood witch." Indeed, she is a solitary, old woman living in a decrepit house, haunted by her past. Yet when the young woman moves in next door, Astrid takes notice. She watches from her window as Veronika emerges for her daily walks, and when several days pass without Veronika's appearing, Astrid feels a newfound sense of concern. Surprising even herself, she goes over to Veronika's house and, finding the woman sick with fever, Astrid makes her pancakes and tea. From that day forward, neither of their lives will be the same.

Astrid begins to join Veronika on her walks, sharing her knowledge of the landscape while also beginning to reveal the painful secrets of her life. At last, she seems to have found the confidant she's always needed but never had. When she divulges that her husband is dying in a rest home nearby, Astrid also reveals the details of her loveless marriage, her once fierce desire for revenge, as well as a terrible confession that shocks her new friend. Veronika doesn't react with indignation or disgust; instead she responds with her own story of love, loss, and guilt. But as she tells Astrid about the tragic death of her fiancé, she also begins to remember the happiness of falling in love.

As winter approaches again, Veronika feels it is time to take the next step in the journey of her life. Astrid agrees, and for herself believes it is also a time to move on. Her friendship with Veronika has given her the chance to care and, in return, get her life back; she has discovered that human connection can heal even a wound so deep that she thought she would never feel again. From Astrid, Veronika has learned to look for the beauty and the joy in all things, and, most importantly, she has realized that remembering, no matter how painful, can bring peace.

Two women, one whose life is only partly written and one whose story is coming to an end, help each other close one chapter of their lives and open the next. Through Astrid, Veronika has uncovered the story she needs to tell in her novel. As she had planned, it is about the power of love, but surprisingly it is not about her fiancé; that book will come later. This one will be about Astrid, who, in helping Veronika discover her story, writes the perfect ending to her own.

A CONVERSATION WITH LINDA OLSSON

1. You have taken a very interesting path to becoming a writer. Would you discuss how you went from a career in banking and finance to becoming a novelist?

Oh, I wouldn't describe it as "went," which sounds quite purposeful. Rather, I found myself having written this book without quite knowing how it happened. Each step on the way seemed so insignificant at the time: taking my first creative writing course in London, writing those first terrible short stories, applying to do a BA in English literature when I arrived in New Zealand, sending a story to the *Sunday Star Times* Short Story Competition. And winning. Then, applying to the new postgraduate course "Writing the Novel." And writing one. And getting it published. I look back and can see a pattern, sort of. But at the time it felt more like ambling along. Living.

2. Veronika talks about "moving from the small streams and ponds of poetry and short stories to the ocean of a novel" (p. 43). Does this reflect your own feelings about writing your first novel? What was this process like for you?

Yes, absolutely. A short story, though I think it is the finest literary art form, is manageable. Things going well, it can be created in one sweeping inspired movement. With a novel, that inspiration will have to be kept alive over an extended period of time. There were several moments during the writing of my novel where I felt ready to put it all aside, to give up. Those dreadful moments when the parts never seemed to become a whole, and it all felt like a presumptuous idea that I should never have acted on. Now, I have enormous respect for the novel as an art form, and I will treat novels that come my way with respect for the sheer craft.

3. The landscapes of both Sweden and New Zealand are very powerful forces in Astrid & Veronika. *How does each place influence you, and how important are place and landscape to you in your work?*

The physical place is very important to me, perhaps because I have moved so much. Someone has been quoted as saying that "those who have traveled much know that place is nothing." I disagree. The more I travel, the more I know where I belong, the more important place becomes. Physical longing for my native

4

Sweden increases year by year, while I know that the longer I live in my present place of residence, New Zealand, the more roots I put down there, too. Also, there is the sense that distance enhances one's appreciation of a remembered place.

4. You've dedicated the novel to your grandmother Anna-Lisa. Would you be willing to share with readers a little bit about her and how she serves as an inspiration to you?

My grandmother was an orphan and I think that all her life she was searching for a connection with something always out of reach. She was oddly out of place wherever she went and always dreamed of a better life. I think that perhaps she gave me a little of those dreams, and when I was the first member of the family to go to university, she was very proud. It felt as if she saw in me the person she would have liked to be, as if I was given the opportunities she would have liked. And that she was so very happy for me. She was the one who taught me about classical music, opera, and ballet. Fine food and fine French wines. All things that were alien to the people I was surrounded by in the working class environment where I grew up. When my grandmother was fifty she followed her son to the United States, perhaps still searching. I longed for her daily, hoping that she would return, but didn't meet her again till I was an adult, when I first visited her in her home in Anaheim, California. One evening, we cooked together. Grandmother made her famous blueberry pie and I my fish soup. As we stood in her kitchen, she suddenly looked up from her work. "It's a pity we are not the same age, you and I," she said. "We would be the best of friends." I looked back at her and said, "We are."

Later, we sat on her small balcony watching the hummingbirds feed on the hibiscus below. I asked if she was ever homesick for Sweden. She looked at me and was silent for a moment. "Always," she said. "I am always homesick." I asked if she would allow me to pay for her to go back and visit Sweden. Again, she was silent. "No, Linda," she said after a while. "I want to remember it as it was. I like my longing. I need it." And she never returned.

Years later, I woke up in my house in Auckland, New Zealand, filled with an intense dream. I had dreamed that my grandmother lay by my side in my bed. She was naked and vulnerable and I pulled her toward me, tucking the bed sheets around us and holding her in my arms. A moment later my aunt rang from California to say that my grandmother had died that night.

Whenever I think of my grandmother, I am filled with an intense feeling of gratitude for having been her granddaughter. And best friend.

5. Most readers probably don't know that you've also written travel books and are quite an adept photographer. How does your travel and photography influence your fiction writing?

I write about places I know, as I think all writers do. It has been my privilege to travel extensively, and get to know many places. I have come to realize that places are both similar and utterly different. People go about their lives all over the world, and it is easy to find connections. Yet, I do think that the place where one spends one's early life will become ingrained in a way that no other place later in life can. We will carry with us the smells, the light, the seasons of our childhood, and it will be the measure against which we will compare all other places we encounter. There is a young woman who works at the checkout in the local supermarket in Auckland where I live. We have gotten to know each other a little and always chat for while when we meet. One day I had bought a couple of mangoes. She took one in her hand and said longingly "These are not as sweet as the mangoes in my country." When I asked her where she was from she said Afghanistan. And added that she would never be able to go back. But the mangoes there are sweeter than anywhere else . . .

6. You are fluent in both Swedish and English and have written in both languages. What impact does the language a novel is written in have on its nature? What specific differences, if any, do you find between your writing in Swedish and in English?

I think that my English writing is more deliberate. That I choose my words more carefully when I write in English. This also means that I see more opportunities in the language. That I am conscious of the impact of each word. Writing in Swedish is more intuitive, I think.

When my book was first released in New Zealand, several of the reviews mentioned that the language sounded "Scandinavian." I once read an article about research that proved that it is possible to discern the composer's native language from the music he or she writes. So, perhaps, in a similar manner, I write in Swedish even when I write in English.

When my book was published in Sweden, I did not translate the book to Swedish myself. I made an attempt, but quickly realized that I was rewriting, rather than translating. For me, it felt as if the story I had written could not just be translated word by word, but that a Swedish version needed other, different expressions. I am enormously grateful that my translator was able to do what I could not.

7. The emotional power of Astrid and Veronika's friendship leaves a lasting impression with readers. They are from different generations and have led very different lives, yet the bond of being women seems to override all else. Do you agree? Do you think that women have different, or deeper, friendships than men? Could this book have been about two men? In what ways would it have been different?

I would like to think that it could just as well have been a story of two men. I have had many interesting responses from male readers, proving that they have reacted deeply and emotionally to the story. If it is true that women have more, and more intense friendships than men, then I think that is due to social roles and behaviors that have been imposed on us more than anything else. I think that more interesting than the gender issue, though, is that of age. In modern Western societies contact between the generations has diminished. There are a number of reasons for this, but sadly it is further encouraged by segregated living and age related categorization. Personally, I find it much easier to relate to young people now than I did when I was in my thirties or forties. Also, it has been a privilege for me to go back to university as a student and find that my fellow students in their early twenties have no issues with my age, while in many other parts of society I am foremost a woman of a certain age.

8. What books or writers have been particularly influential in your life? What are you reading now?

This is such a difficult question—a bit like being asked what food has made your body what it is today. I have been a voracious and indiscriminate reader since I first learnt to read. Just as with food, I like anything as long as it is made from good ingredients and well cooked. I grew up on a mix of Swedish and Anglo-Saxon literature, I suppose. And that is still my staple literary nourishment. Saul Bellow, Philip Roth, and Paul Auster are some of my favorites. I like short stories very much and Alice Munro is a particular favorite. I keep coming back to August Strindberg, the only Swedish author of international significance. Among the classics I am particularly fond of Gogol and Kafka. I like a good thriller, and there are a number of superb Swedish writers who are among the best in the world in this genre: Henning Mankell, Roslund and Hellström, Stieg Larsson. And I read more and more poetry.

For my next book I am doing quite a bit of research, reading essays and books on modern Polish history.

9. What are you working on next?

First, my new novel has a male main character. I am conscious of the challenge of creating a believable male voice, but in a sense, as it was with Astrid and Veronika, it has been him choosing me, not the other way around. He has appeared in my life and I am trying to write his story as well as I can. Again, I am interested in the issue of relationships between people, how we choose to relate, or not to relate to each other. I want to explore the consequences of silence. And that is also the working title on my new novel: "The Consequence of Silence."

QUESTIONS FOR DISCUSSION

1. Astrid has been solitary for so long. Why, then, do you think she is drawn to Veronika, essentially a stranger, and then later allows herself to open up to her so freely?

2. The houses in the novel serve almost as characters. The author describes Astrid's house as "dark and warm . . . It was an organic part of her and its shapes were ingrained in her body" (p. 9). Discuss how the author uses the houses in the novel. What is the importance of a home in our lives? How does our house/living space define us? What do you think your house/living space says about you?

3. Astrid's mother committed suicide when Astrid was six years old; Veronika's mother left when Veronika was a child. Talk about the theme of the "absent mother" and how it influences these characters' lives.

4. What did you think of Astrid's confession regarding the death of her child? Were you able to understand her actions? Did knowing this about her past affect the way you felt about her? What do you think Astrid expected Veronika's reaction would be to her story? Was Astrid taking a risk in telling her? Why do you think Veronika reacts in the way she does?

5. Veronika feels very guilty about the death of her fiancé and agonizes over what she could have done differently that day to prevent his death. Why do you think she feels so guilty?

6. When Astrid tries on the floral swimsuit during Veronika's birthday "outing," the women burst out into laughter (p. 85). Why do the women find this moment so hysterically funny? How does this day, Veronika's birthday, serve as a turning point in the novel?

7. After her husband dies, Astrid says to Veronika, "There was nothing more to be afraid of. . . . It was never about him. It was about me" (p.167). What does she mean?

8. Veronika visits her father after her fiancé's death, and when she is leaving her father begins to say, "I wish . . ." but doesn't complete the sentence (p. 200). What do you think he was going to say? How would you describe Veronika's relationship with him?

9. Great literary novels skillfully incorporate sometimes elaborate symbolism. In *Astrid & Veronika*, Olsson makes repeated and significant references to water. Discuss the symbolic function of water in the novel and consider how water may be connected with Olsson's major themes.

10. Discuss how the seasons shape the novel. How do the seasons influence the characters? Discuss the ways that the seasons affect

you throughout the year. Are your memories connected to the seasons in which they took place?

11. In her letter to Veronika, Astrid mentions "a great love" (p. 241). Whom do you think she is talking about?

For more information about or to order other Penguin Readers Guides, please e-mail the Penguin Marketing Department at reading@us.penguingroup.com or write to us at:

Penguin Books Marketing Dept.
Readers Guides
375 Hudson Street
New York, NY 10014-3657

Please allow 4–6 weeks for delivery.
To access Penguin Readers Guides online, visit the Penguin Group (USA) Web site at www.penguin.com.

FOR THE BEST IN PAPERBACKS, LOOK FOR THE

In every corner of the world, on every subject under the sun, Penguin represents quality and variety—the very best in publishing today.

For complete information about books available from Penguin—including Penguin Classics and Puffins—and how to order them, write to us at the appropriate address below. Please note that for copyright reasons the selection of books varies from country to country.

In the United States: Please write to *Penguin Group (USA), P.O. Box 12289 Dept. B, Newark, New Jersey 07101-5289* or call *1-800-788-6262*.

In the United Kingdom: Please write to *Dept. EP, Penguin Books Ltd, Bath Road, Harmondsworth, West Drayton, Middlesex UB7 0DA*.

In Canada: Please write to *Penguin Books Canada Ltd, 90 Eglinton Avenue East, Suite 700, Toronto, Ontario M4P 2Y3*.

In Australia: Please write to *Penguin Books Australia Ltd, P.O. Box 257, Ringwood, Victoria 3134*.

In New Zealand: Please write to *Penguin Books (NZ) Ltd, Private Bag 102902, North Shore Mail Centre, Auckland 10*.

In India: Please write to *Penguin Books India Pvt Ltd, 11 Panchsheel Shopping Centre, Panchsheel Park, New Delhi 110 017*.

In the Netherlands: Please write to *Penguin Books Netherlands bv, Postbus 3507, NL-1001 AH Amsterdam*.

In Germany: Please write to *Penguin Books Deutschland GmbH, Metzlerstrasse 26, 60594 Frankfurt am Main*.

In Spain: Please write to *Penguin Books S. A., Bravo Murillo 19, 1° B, 28015 Madrid*.

In Italy: Please write to *Penguin Italia s.r.l., Via Benedetto Croce 2, 20094 Corsico, Milano*.

In France: Please write to *Penguin France, Le Carré Wilson, 62 rue Benjamin Baillaud, 31500 Toulouse*.

In Japan: Please write to *Penguin Books Japan Ltd, Kaneko Building, 2-3-25 Koraku, Bunkyo-Ku, Tokyo 112*.

In South Africa: Please write to *Penguin Books South Africa (Pty) Ltd, Private Bag X14, Parkview, 2122 Johannesburg*.